Enjoy with my
best wishes
Di Johnson

Wagons to Hangtown

Also by Diana M. Johnson

Charlemagne Trilogy
Destiny's Godchild
Pepin's Bastard
Quest for the Crown

Colonial Virginia
Cradle of a Nation

Historical Fiction for Middle School Readers
Will & Davy

Wagons to Hangtown

A story of the California Gold Rush

Diana M. Johnson

SUPERIOR BOOK PUBLISHING COMPANY
North Hills, California

Superior Book Publishing Company
16417 Superior Street
North Hills, CA 91343-1836

Library of Congress Cataloging-in-Publication Data
Johnson, Diana M.
Wagons to Hangtown, A story of the California Gold Rush: a novel/Diana M. Johnson

1.Edward Brochenbrough Daingerfield, born 17 April 1826, Winchester Co. VA, died 23 July 1921, Pacific Grove, CA, arrived Hangtown (Placerville), CA 20 August 1850, worked in the Placerville Post Office ca. 1852 - 1854, drove stage for Barton & Ellison, 1854, editor Volcano Ledger in association with Thomas A. Springer 1855 - 1857, witnessed the hanging of Mickey Free and Jerry Crane 26 October 1855, Coloma, CA, married Miss Ellen Logan 1 January 1857, Clarksville, CA, drove stage with Horace Greeley from Sportsmans Hill to Placerville—Fiction. 2. Richard W. Chenowith (cousin?) born VA, listed in 1850 Placerville census living with Edward B. Daingerfield—Fiction. 3. Lewis H. Rudesill (friend?) born IN, listed in 1850 Placerville census living with Edward B. Daingerfield, married Elizabeth M. Priest, 21 February 1853, Putnam County, IN—Fiction. 4. Thomas Carr Nugent, born 1822, southeastern IN, died Berkeley, CA, Post Master Placerville, 9 April 1850—Fiction.

Library of Congress Control Number: 2010921172
ISBN 978-0-9661504-6-9

Author photograph by William R. Johnson
Cover Design© Howard Goldstein
Printed in the USA

To the memory of my great-great-aunt Edith Daingerfield, who did the initial research tracing our family back to Charlemagne

My friend & fellow author JoAnn Levy, an expert on the California Gold Rush

And always, my love, Bill

Acknowledgements

The newspaper articles I read in researching Edward Brochenbrough Daingerfield quote him as saying, "I arrived in Hangtown (Placerville) at age 22, on August 20, 1850, and the first entertainment I saw was a bull and bear fight on Main Street."

And that's where I planned to start my story, until my husband said, "We've got to know where he came from. And what he went through to get to California."

I realized Bill was absolutely right. I knew E.B. was born in Virginia and moved to Indiana with his family when he was eight, but I knew nothing about the town of Greencastle, Indiana.

I asked my genealogical guru, Dee Rickards, and she suggested I search the Daughters of the American Revolution, Greencastle, Indiana website. I did, and found a phone number and email address for Regent Jinsie Scott Bingham, Greencastle Chapter, DAR. I emailed, and told her I was an author who writes historical fiction based on members of my family tree. I needed to find out everything about Greencastle from 1848—when my great-great-grandfather, Edward (E.B.) Daingerfield heard about the California Gold

Rush—to 1850 when he left home for California. And then I needed later information, about which his family might well have written him.

Jinsie sent me the historical information she knew about Greencastle, and gave me a phone number for Linda Ford of the *Fine Print Bookstore*, from whom I might be able to purchase a copy of the *1879 Putman County Atlas.* She also sent me to the Putnam County Library Family History Room for genealogical research.

Not only did Linda sell me the illustrated atlas, she got me in touch with John Baughman, a retired history professor from Greencastle's DePauw University (formerly Indiana Asbury University, organized in 1837). Between them I had found a gold mine of historical information about the town, including the fact that E.B. Daingerfield was a student at Asbury University, but didn't graduate.

Meanwhile, Susan Harmon, librarian of the Family History Room, and Rick Monroe, Reference Assistant, Local History Department of the Putnam County Public Library, provided invaluable genealogical and historical information on Greencastle, Indiana.

In the final draft, my editor advised me to begin with the journey itself. "This is where the story gets 'rolling'," she said. "Then fill in what came before in some judicious flashbacks."

For the covered wagon trip to California, I knew exactly where to turn. My friend and former writing critique group member, JoAnn Levy, authored the landmark nonfiction book, *They Saw the Elephant, Women in the California*

Gold Rush. Through her book, I learned of *The Emigrants' Guide to California,* by Joseph E. Ware. A 1932 reprint of the original 1849 edition could be ordered through our local public library.

With those two books as reference, I knew exactly where Edward would have gone, what he would have seen, and how he would have felt, every step of the way to California. I also checked the Internet for every stop, and found photographs and diary excerpts to further personalize my great-great-grandfather's story.

That story, of crossing the continent in 1850, was longer, harder, more dangerous, and sadder—but often more beautiful—than I ever could have imagined.

Once I got E.B. to Hangtown, the research was much easier. Bill's mother had moved to Sutter Creek, a small town in California's Mother Lode, in 1970. We read the local newspaper *Jackson Ledger Dispatch* every time we visited her. When she passed away, and we needed to advertise a yard sale prior to selling her house, we advertised it in that newspaper.

By the time I was ready to begin preliminary research for this book, we went to the *Ledger's* office and asked, "Is the *Jackson Ledger Dispatch* the same paper as the old *Volcano Ledger* that became *Jackson Ledger?"*

When the lady at the counter said, "Yes," I said, "I think my great-great-grandfather started your paper."

The lady looked doubtful but asked, "What was his name?" I answered, "Edward Brochenbrough Daingerfield."

"Oh, yes," she answered, "we know *all* about him."

Larry Cenotto, former archivist of the Amador County Archives, made all the back issues of the *Ledger* available for us to photocopy and/or transcribe for my research.

Bill and I trekked all over the Mother Lode, to libraries and museums in Jackson, Placerville, and Volcano; and then to Gilroy and Pacific Grove. Everywhere we went we met delightfully helpful people. We were even invited into the home in Pacific Grove where this book begins and ends, thanks to owner, Rennie Lane Agee.

Daingerfield was twenty when he heard about the discovery of gold in California, twenty-two when he arrived. He lived here another seventy years. When I started, I had no idea where my story would end, so I collected thick notebooks stuffed with information. I had help from Lucy Solorzano, Jr., and Erin E. Griesbaum of the Gilroy Historical Museum, Adam Weiland of The Heritage Society of Pacific Grove, Ann Adler, Librarian, Santa Clara County Historical and Genealogical Society, and State DAR Chaplain, Ann Zuhr of Gilroy.

Sandy Krutelik, a fellow member of both Conejo Valley Chapter DAR and First California Company Jamestowne Society visited with me about the California Gold Rush historical novel I was writing. She offered to loan me her treasured copy of *Discovery of the Yosemite in 1851,* by one of the participants, Lafayette Houghton Bunnell, M.D. of the Mariposa Battalion. Reading it, I immediately decided to borrow from Bunnell's story, turning it into a newspaper article in Chapter Thirty-Seven of this book.

When Edward received word that his sister Eliza had died in Greencastle, I felt he might have suffered a loss of faith—so far from home and caught up in the whirlwind of gold fever. I remembered a sermon by Pastor Jim Sillerud of First Presbyterian Church of Granada Hills, *When God is Silent.* I thank him for allowing me to paraphrase this sermon for Chapter Forty-Five.

When I needed information on Edward's partner in starting the *Volcano Ledger*, Thomas A. Springer, Deborah Cook of *The Time Detective, Professional Historic Research Services,* came to the rescue.

With every book, I must acknowledge the help and support of my writing critique group, Howard Goldstein—friend, fellow writer, and cover artist—Ester Benjamin Shifren, Dolly Wiseman, and former members, Millie Grey and Jean Akers. I wouldn't think of writing a book without you guys watching my back. Nor would I begin, without the sure knowledge that Tina (Farrell) Glasner would be my editor. Her comments, questions, and suggestions make a huge difference between first and final draft.

And finally, my love, admiration, and gratitude go to Bill, who is with me every step of the way. Friend, love of my life, first reader, last reader, photographer, and business partner—I can't imagine life without him.

Diana M. Johnson
billndi@verizon.net

Wagons to Hangtown

Prologue

Pacific Grove, 1920

Edward looked up from trimming his roses as the mail boy opened the gate.

"Letter for you, Mr. Daingerfield."

Wiping the dirt off his hands, Edward took the offered heavy cream envelope. Beautiful calligraphy spelled out:

Mr. Edward Brochenbrough Daingerfield
302 17th Street
Pacific Grove, California

Inside, the Association of California State Newspaper Editors invited him to be the honored guest and featured speaker for their upcoming convention at Asilomar Conference Center, Pacific Grove. They were most interested in hearing, from his own lips, "the adventures of a participant as well as a newspaper editor, during the California Gold Rush."

"Ellen! Ellen come see this," he called.

Upon reading the message, she smiled. "That's quite an honor, E.B., but that was, what… seventy years ago. Do you even remember those days?"

Taking her hand in his, he said, "As if it were yesterday, my dear. As if it were but yesterday…"

Chapter One

Saint Joseph Missouri,
Tuesday, April 23, 1850

Edward gripped the rail of the paddle wheeler as it churned toward the wharf at St. Joseph. He had expected to feel exhilarated. Thrilled.

He looked around. Shook his head.

"My God!" he exclaimed, dropping to his knees on top of their possessions, packed around them. "*This* is St. Jo?"

"It certainly isn't Greencastle, Indiana," his cousin Richard Chenoweth commiserated.

"It's *worse* than Independence," his friend Lewis Rudesill declared. "I *knew* we should have gotten off there. Didn't I say so? I *told* you we should buy our wagon and oxen in Independence, but oh, no! *You* knew so much better!"

Lewis' face was nearly as red as his hair. "*Now* what are we going to do?"

Richard took charge, as he always did. "We're going to do exactly what we all agreed to. You'll stay on the wharf with our baggage while E.B. and I go looking for a wheelbarrow or handcart. Then, together we'll search for a covered wagon and oxen to buy. Once the wagon's loaded, and we buy the rest of our supplies, we'll get a ticket for the ferry to cross the river and... go to California! Find gold! Get rich!

❊ ❊ ❊

"It *is* an ugly, dirty town," Richard admitted a while later, as he pushed a rickety handcart back to the wharf.

Edward, dismayed, stared at groups of men playing poker practically in the middle of the street. "Why aren't they *doing* something? *Going* somewhere?"

Inquiring of a group of idlers, they were told everyone was waiting for the prairie grass across the river to turn green. Until then, the wagon trains couldn't get underway because there would be nothing for the livestock to eat. In fact, no more wagons were being allowed across the river until then. To everyone's dismay, spring came late in 1850.

After returning to Lewis, the three of them, all their worldly goods on their backs or in the overloaded handcart, went to the ferry office to purchase a ticket and get a numbered boarding pass.

"Number *twenty-seven?*" Lewis exploded. "It'll be *summer* by the time we start across the prairie." He grabbed Richard's arm, but taller and heavier, Richard easily shook him off.

"Calm down. We need to get a wagon and team. Buy supplies. Find out where we're supposed to wait."

Edward merely smiled at the outbreak. Lewis had an enviable temper. On the other hand, there was no more loyal friend. "Getting mad at the world won't help," he said. Though he, too, felt discouraged.

What they found did nothing to cheer them up. Only mules could be had for the little money the three had allotted for the purchase of a team of oxen.

"People who brought their wagons from home, must have sold their mules here," Edward said.

"They *sold* them, because mules can't survive the desert, or have the strength to haul a wagon up the mountains," Lewis reminded them. "They're worthless to us, too."

They went to another stockyard. "Look, there are some great looking oxen!" cried Edward, his spirits rising. "Let's get those four."

The oxen stood in a separate area from the rest of the animals. Huge beasts, obviously well fed, their golden coats shone in the sunshine.

But when they asked the stockman, he said, "Yep. Them's good oxen. Best to be had in all of St. Jo. One hundred dollars apiece."

Edward felt as though he had been punched in the stomach. Looking at the others, he saw them equally shocked.

"But, but..." Lewis sputtered.

"That's *twice* the cost we were told." Richard looked angry.

"Oh-ho, you've been reading that Ware book, *Emigrants' Guide to California*, or some such, ain't ya?" He wiped his brow with a dirty rag.

"Well you can have them four over *there* for fifty dollars apiece." The stockman pointed to four gaunt animals looking so old they probably couldn't walk out of town on their own, let alone pull a wagon all the way to California.

"But, we can't afford a hundred apiece, and we can't possibly plan to use *those*." Edward pointed at the feeble-looking four.

"You don't pay a hundred apiece, someone else will." The stockman turned to walk away.

"Wait. Wait a minute," called Richard. "Let us discuss this among ourselves. Just don't sell them until we do."

"Make it snappy," the stockman growled. "There's plenty more buyers coming." He continued walking back to his office.

"What'll we do?" asked Lewis. "The oxen and wagon are the most important items on our list. We can't go anywhere without strong animals."

"True," answered Richard. "But we can't spend twice as much for everything we need to buy. Especially not right at the beginning."

"I *told* you we should have gotten off at Independence!"

Richard's face flushed, but he held his temper. "Do you want to go back?"

"No, I don't want to go back!" Lewis shouted. "I want to have bought our supplies at Independence and be over half-way here with good livestock."

"So, go back!"

"No!" Lewis clenched his fists.

"Shut up!" Edward shouted. "Both of you!"

In the sudden shocked silence that followed, Edward declared with vehemence, "We *need* these oxen."

"Think there are any *other* strong healthy oxen in St. Joseph?" asked Richard, without much hope.

"Maybe." Lewis' voice dropped. "Probably not."

"We can't pay four hundred dollars for these." Edward was adamant.

"Everything—oxen, wagon, supplies—was supposed to cost only *six* hundred," Richard reminded them.

Silence.

Edward thought of all time they had spent in planning; the preparations they had made. Suddenly with a smile and a little jig, he announced, "I've got a plan!"

Chapter Two

For a breathless moment the three young men stood transfixed, as if in a tableaux.

Then Edward beckoned them closer. When he spoke his voice was barely above a whisper. "We are *not* going to pay four hundred dollars for oxen—at least not in cash. But what if we offered him two hundred dollars, which we planned on spending anyway, and added something of even greater value than money?"

"What do *we* have that's of greater value than money?" asked Richard.

"If your child is sick," Edward responded, "what would you rather have, a hundred dollars or the medicine to make him well?"

"You... you mean the pharmaceuticals your father insisted we take with us?" asked Richard.

Edward nodded. "At first I didn't want to take them. Remember what Ware said in his book?"

"Don't take large quantities of medicines," Lewis recited. "'Cleanliness and frequent bathing are your best preventives of sickness.'"

"Right! Not that Father, as Greencastle's pharmacist, would adhere to that doctrine."

"But what does that have to do with buying the oxen?" asked Lewis. "With a hundred dollars that guy could buy all the pharmaceuticals he wants."

"Remember how expensive drugs were, as close to home as St. Louis?" Edward reminded them. "And what if they don't have what you're convinced you need here? I'll bet medicines are *very* expensive—if you can even get them in this town."

The other two began to nod their heads and smile.

"Now, here's my idea..."

Edward looked each one in the eyes, and then outlined his plan.

When he finished they shook hands and stood up, smiling.

"Remember," Edward reminded them, "look concerned."

"Yes," Lewis agreed. "We *really* don't want to part with any of our drugs, do we?"

When the stockman returned, Richard said, "I'll tell you what we are willing to do. We realize these oxen are prime animals, and no doubt worth every penny you're asking. But, we simply can't afford to pay it."

The stockman started to walk away saying, "Well, it don't make no never-mind to—"

"But," Richard interrupted. "We *do* have an idea."

The stockman turned back.

"We have some very precious medicines, which we really need to take with us if we are to survive the journey," Richard continued.

Edward picked up the conversation. "When you get sick, no amount of money will do, if you can't buy what you need to make you well."

The stockman looked interested. "What do you have?"

"Well, we've got calomel—"

"What's that for?"

"It's a purgative," Edward said. "Eliminates parasitic worms. And also stimulates the organs, especially the liver."

The stockman nodded his head. "That sounds good."

"How about if we gave you two hundred dollars *and* two packets of calomel for the four oxen?" Richard asked.

The stockman looked tempted, but shook his head. "Two hundred dollars and *four* packets of calomel!"

"For that," Edward responded, "we should get the four oxen *and* the best wagon in St. Jo!"

The stockman thought a moment, then with a sly look asked, "What else you got in that there hand cart of yourn?"

"Well," Edward admitted with reluctance, "we *do* have laudanum to relieve pain and camphor balls to ward off illness..."

"Two hundred dollars, four calomel, and *four each* of the laudanum and camphor, and it's a deal!"

Richard shook his head. "Two hundred dollars, four calomel, and *two* packages each of laudanum and camphor balls. Not one more thing!"

A long silence ensued as the stockman considered the offer. Finally, nodding again, he spat in his hand, then stuck it our. “Deal!”

They all looked at the huge, dirty, work-roughened paw. After a moment’s hesitation, Richard gingerly offered his own.

Lewis put in the final word. “It better be the *best* wagon in town. We don’t want to hitch those beautiful animals to anything less.”

Chapter Three

"You should be the first one to drive the wagon," Richard said to Edward as they finished loading their gear.

"Me?" Edward shook his head in surprise. "You're the leader of our expedition."

"But, you had the idea that saved the day."

Edward stood taller. "By gosh, I did, didn't I?"

Sitting in the driver's seat, he picked up the reins. The four strongly muscled oxen began pulling the brand new wagon, its white, painted canvas top gleaming in the late afternoon sun, down the main street of St. Joseph.

Men, women, and children paused to goggle at the magnificent animals and wagon as they passed. Heads turned. Eyes grew wide. Everyone seemed to recognize the oxen, and took a second look to see who was driving.

Edward nodded, tipped the brim of his slouch hat, acknowledging their stares. He brandished the whip, not daring to actually snap it and cause a stampede in the crowded streets.

As they approached the wharf where the line had formed to board the steamer across the Missouri River, his pride melted into dismay. The line stretched away from the river, through several blocks of town, and out the other side, far into the prairie.

Edward felt smaller with each plodding hoof fall and each rotation of the wooden wheels.

On and on, following the track, he counted the wagons they passed, "...twenty-three, twenty-four, twenty-five, ...

"Are you wagon number twenty-six?"

"Yup," answered a man who was rummaging through his supplies. "You number twenty-seven?"

Edward showed him their boarding pass. Then snapping the whip over the oxen, and pulling hard on the right reins, he shouted, "Gee!"

Their wagon had taken its place at the end of the long, long line.

Edward climbed down, joining Richard and Lewis who had walked with the wagon.

The man from number twenty-six sauntered over to meet them. "Name's Gould," he said holding out a hand.

"I'm Edward, my cousin Richard, and best friend Lewis."

"I figured you two for brothers," Gould said, indicating Edward and Richard.

Edward guessed they did have a family resemblance—light brown hair and blue eyes. He was slightly taller and thinner than Richard. They both usually had well-trimmed moustaches, but after two weeks of travel they had grown short beards as well.

"An' this here's the missus, and Ellen," Gould said as mother and daughter came over to join the group.

Edward tipped his hat as he said, "Missus Gould. Ellen." He had to smile at the little girl. She looked to be about the same age as his brother Lawrence, and he felt a stab of homesickness for the family he'd left behind.

"Looks like Ol' Charlie finally sold his prize winnin' oxen."

"Yes," Edward admitted, without elaboration.

"Whatever you paid, they should at least see you to California."

"We certainly hope so." The boys had agreed; it was nobody's business how they had paid for the oxen and wagon. It would be no help to brag—or have everyone aware they still had precious pharmaceuticals in their wagon.

"Do you have any idea how long it will be before they let us start?" Richard asked.

"Whenever the prairie grass greens up. Then, they'll only let us cross, a few at a time. Need to keep us spread out, so's we don't overgraze. Prairie *looks* big enough, but we all want to head straight west so's we don't run out of supplies.

"Where are you all from?" Gould asked.

Richard, taking leadership for their wagon, answered for them.

"Greencastle, Indiana. How about you?"

"Same general direction. Cincinnati, Ohio."

With another handshake, the Goulds left, and the three began setting up camp as people had done by every wagon up the long line snaking its way into St. Jo.

They used the next week to take turns going into St. Jo to buy more supplies. Besides their sleeping tent, they got an extra tent for eating in, and a sheet iron stove whose pipe went through a hole in the tent, just like one Edward had admired in St. Louis. Rain or shine, they could cook up beans, soup, or coffee without getting wet.

Lewis sewed muslin into sacks to store supplies, boxes being too cumbersome and heavy for the long journey. Dried fruit and nuts joined the supplies, as did blankets and kettles. Equipment included rope, stakes to tie down the oxen at night, chains, axes, and carpenter's tools. They happily found a 20-gallon wooden cask for water.

They also bought barrels of flour, bacon, coffee, sugar, rice, beans, molasses, and vinegar. And hay for their prize-winning oxen, while they waited for the prairie to green up.

Edward slaughtered and roasted chickens, and fried up eggs to eat while they were encamped. In the days ahead, they would remember the taste of fresh meat and winter vegetables with longing.

Chapter Four

While waiting, the three had become friends, not only with the Goulds, but also with several wagons around them.

Edward never heard the Goulds address each other in any way but, 'Mr. Gould' and 'Mrs. Gould'. He was slender, with a receding hairline and sideburns beginning to turn gray. She was a plump, motherly woman, with a dimple, and a twinkle in her blue eyes. Ellen turned out to be ten, shy, but obedient and helpful around the wagon.

The wagon ahead of the Gould's, number twenty-five, held William and Nancy Kelsey from St. Louis, and their two young children, Lucy, five and Caleb, four. Edward looked on with amusement as Ellen took it upon herself to entertain the toddlers. She'll make a good mother one of these days, he thought.

Behind Edward's wagon came Samuel Wilson and his fifteen-year-old son George. Samuel had left his wife and two daughters back in Kentucky. Edward couldn't begin to imagine a father leaving half his immediate family behind. Dark-haired, blue-eyed George was at a halfway-in-between age. Sometimes wanting to play like a child, but mostly acting like he was going on twenty.

Behind the Wilsons came two brothers, John Cummings, eighteen, and Benjamin, twenty-one, from Pittsburg, Pennsylvania. Fifteen-year-old George Wilson followed John around like a puppy, when he wasn't teasing Ellen.

Last in the group that had all become friends and had decided to stick together in whatever wagon train they ended up, were Frank and Mary Ann Ashley. They were young. In love. And even under her full skirt and ample apron, obviously expecting a child. Mrs. Gould clucked and mothered Mary Ann as if she were her very own.

* * *

Late one evening, Edward and Gould were the only ones sitting by the Gould's campfire, sipping a last cup of coffee. The rest of their group were already sound asleep, wrapped in their bedrolls. Looking up and down the line of over forty wagons, stretching far out into the prairie from St. Jo, Edward saw half a dozen similar fires twinkling golden in the blackness.

"How did you first hear about the gold discovery in California?" asked Gould.

Edward paused, thinking back. "I know it was in June of '48. I'd just finished my freshman year at Indiana Asbury University, and had a summer job at *The Argus,* our town newspaper. John Turk, the owner and editor had hired me as a cub reporter—really just a glorified errand boy.

"I'd just picked up the mail, and there in a copy of the *St. Louis Union* was a full-page article about how James Marshall had discovered gold. The paper said he was operating a lumber mill in a small town in the California foothills named Coloma. It was evening, and he'd redirected the water from running the wheel that powered the saw, and there in the tail race he saw bright, malleable nuggets."

"Yep, that was the same information we received, when the St. Louis papers reached Cincinnati," Gould remarked.

"What's sort of humorous, thinking back on it now," Edward continued, "is how my family reacted to the news at dinner that night. I mentioned the *St. Louis Union* article and..."

* * *

"Where's California?" asked ten-year-old Lawrence.

Eliza, fourteen, said, "Why, it's all the way across the continent. On the edge of the Pacific Ocean."

"How far is that?" Lawrence persisted.

"Goodness, I don't know." Eliza returned to the fresh string beans on her plate.

"You'd have to cross, I can't even guess, how many rivers," Edward contributed, "and days and days of prairies. And after that, mountains so tall, they make the Appalachians we crossed coming here from Virginia look like little lumps in the ground."

At Lawrence's look of incomprehension, Edward added. "Of course, you weren't born until after we got to Indiana, so you wouldn't know."

"Does California still belong to Mexico?" asked Mother.

For one of the first times in his life, Edward felt what he'd learned in school was pertinent to his life today. "No! It doesn't. Just before the end of the semester I heard about it at school. One of the professors mentioned America and

Mexico had signed a treaty ending the Mexican War. Since it wouldn't be on any exams, I didn't take notes. But, if I remember correctly, the signing was in early February. The big deal of it is, the treaty extends the U.S. border all the way to the Pacific Ocean."

After a short pause, Edward blurted, "My gosh! I didn't make the connection until just now. Gold was discovered on January twenty-fourth, and California became a territory of the United States early in February. I bet the Mexicans would have fought harder, if they'd known they had gold right under their feet!"

"Even if they had," Lawrence commented, "the Americans still would have won the war."

Edward smiled and ruffled his loyal younger brother's hair.

Then, his attention was caught by the gleam of the fork in front of him, and he imagined what it would be like to hold a piece of gold he'd just plucked out of a stream, similarly glinting in his hand.

He shook his head. Ate a bite of roasted chicken. He'd never go so far away as California.

***

Edward looked at Gould. "Thinking back on their reaction, it was sort of...

"They've discovered Gold in California."

"Where's California?"

"A long way away."

"Oh. Please pass the string beans."

Chapter Five

When at last the wagons ahead began to move, the air of being on a picnic changed. People folded up tents, packed food and cooking utensils. The children ran in circles with excitement.

Knowing it would take several days for their wagon to work its way to St. Jo and the wharf, Edward spent his time re-reading his journal and writing an article for *The Argus.* He smiled as he skipped the details about how they managed to pay for their wagon and oxen!

Little by little, they inched forward. At the end of each day, they made a fire, cooked supper, and unrolled bedding on the ground beside their wagons. Finally their part of the line was inside the town of St. Jo. Their last day to buy fresh provisions for the journey.

While he was in town, Edward folded and addressed his article. Then he walked it to the post office where it would join the weekly mail service. Once loaded onto a paddle wheeler, for the journey to Independence and St. Louis, his article would then travel overland to Greencastle. With the price of one letter, his whole family—indeed the entire town—would know where he was and that he was fine. And, he would have a byline on the article as well!

After tomorrow, they would be traveling in the Nebraska Territory. No more towns. No more post offices. The rest of his articles, and any letters, would travel on irregularly scheduled U.S. Army supply wagons from the widely scattered forts across the prairie.

❋❋❋

At last, on Wednesday, the first of May, it was their turn to guide the oxen, pulling the wagon, up the gangplank and onto the side-wheeler. The ferryboat was nothing like the grand steamboat they had taken from St. Louis. That ship had had three decks and carried passengers as well as freight up the mighty Mississippi, before turning west on the Missouri River.

The Missouri had served them well as a navigable road west to Independence. From there the river had turned north to St. Jo and beyond. But, they were as far north as they needed to go. Now, to resume journeying westward, they'd have to travel overland.

This ferryboat had but one deck, and could take six covered wagons and their teams per trip. On deck, they lined up, two wagons side by side, and three pairs from bow to stern.

Everyone pressed against the railing, looking out at the wide, slow-moving river. Then, with a bellow from the whistle, and a belch of smoke, the paddles began to turn. The passengers cheered, while onlookers shouted from the dock.

Edward felt the movement of air in his face as the ferry started across the expanse of water. He felt the vibration of the powerful steam engine through the soles of his boots. The giant wheel dug into the water, making it churn and splash. Cascades and droplets sparkled in the sunlight—rare jewels on a splendid day.

"I wonder how many rivers we'll cross, before we get to California?" he murmured.

"All without ferries," added Richard.

"And how many mountains," Lewis said, "without roads?"

They stood, silently taking in the majesty of the broad river...and absorbing the immensity of their undertaking.

Gradually the words and plaintive melody of the popular song *Shenandoah* filled Edward's head.

Away, we're bound away,
Cross the wide Missouri.

Chapter Six

The open prairie beckoned the wagons as they disgorged from the St. Joseph ferry. The grasses were a soft green, dotted here and there with small white or yellow flowers. Overhead, the afternoon sun spread its benediction.

Urged on by the promise of gold, Edward wanted to leave immediately. "This is it! We're finally on our way," he shouted to his companions.

Two wagons, *California or Bust* painted in black letters on the canvas tops, went past them without hesitation.

The six wagons they'd been in line with in St. Jo clustered a few hundred yards up the river. Other groups dotted the landscape.

"Why are we stopping here?" asked Lewis. "Folks like them are going to beat us to the gold fields. There won't be any left for us."

"You read Ware's book," Gould responded. "Organize now and we'll pass their broken-down wagons later on."

"According to the book," Edward said, "we just need to go west for a couple of days to reach the Indian Mission. So, why don't we get a couple of hours' travel in before we make camp?"

However, after conferring, everyone decided to set up camp where they were for now. They'd take off the next morning, following the wagon tracks leading to the Iowa, Sac, and Fox Mission.

"The six of us can leave together when we're ready, and travel at our own speed," Gould suggested. "That way, we'll get used to the routine.

"Once we get to the Mission," he continued, "we'll be ready to join a larger group, elect a captain, and officially form a wagon train."

Lewis led the oxen to graze outside the small circle of six wagons, while Edward started a fire to cook supper, and Richard set up the tent for sleeping.

"Mary Ann," Mrs. Gould said, sounding serious, "you don't want to ride in the wagon in your condition. Walking all the way to California isn't bad for you, but bouncing on a hard wagon bench could be disastrous.

"When your William needs to be spelled from driving the oxen, get one of these handsome young men to give him a break."

"There's three of us," Richard agreed. "Two of us can easily spell each other, while the third one gives your husband a break any time he needs one."

❊❊❊

Up at dawn the next morning, the six wagons filed onto the tracks leading west. Following the same wagons that had camped in line from the St. Joseph wharf, they joined a seeming endless stream of wagons. Only the drivers rode. Everyone else walked. Even little Lucy and Caleb, when they weren't napping on quilts inside. In no time at all, Mrs. Gould and Nancy Kelsey were able to drive their wagons every bit as well as their husbands, who appreciated a break from the bone-crushing jarring of wooden wheels jouncing over the rutted dirt track.

They occasionally saw Indians following the wagons on their small ponies, but so far none had ventured close enough to talk to.

* * *

Two days later, at nearly dark, the wagon train set up camp in a grove of trees surrounding the Indian Mission.

A tall woman in serviceable dark clothing, her graying hair tucked into a bonnet, came to greet the newcomers.

"Welcome! I'm Sarah Warren. My husband, the Reverend Samuel Warren and I established this mission thirteen years ago, to offer Christianity and education to the Indians in the area.

"The Iowa, Sac, and Fox Indians were given this land in exchange for theirs in northeast Kansas and northwest Missouri. If you came through St. Joseph, that was originally their land."

Edward and the other men tipped their hats, while the women each dipped a curtsy, and murmured, "Glad to meet you."

"You and your companions are welcome to come to Sabbath services tomorrow, if you wish," Sarah Warren offered. "They're held in the big building in the clearing. You can't miss it."

* * *

The next morning, Edward, Richard and Lewis stomped the dust off their boots as they entered the handsome three-story, stone-and-brick building. Several others from the large group of wagons had come as well. Much cleaner, more healthy, and better-dressed Indians than those they had seen on the trail, took up the rest of the benches.

Familiar Bible verses and Reverend Warren's sermon transported Edward back to Greencastle.

Mother, Father, Eliza and Lawrence are, right now, sitting in church, hearing words from the very same Book, he thought. If he closed his eyes, he could hear Uncle Alfred, the Reverend Chenoweth, preaching.

And after church, members of the family will gather at our home for dinner, as usual...

❊❊❊

Uncle John Chenoweth, and Aunt Sarah along with their children, came to town from their farm for church on Sunday. Of course Uncle Alfred and Aunt Jane, with their family joined them all for dinner. Since it was Sunday, they used the dining room rather than the kitchen. With all of the leaves in the table, they could seat the whole family together.

"My, doesn't your table look pretty," commented Aunt Sarah. "The roses are especially lovely this summer."

Ellen Chenoweth Daingerfield paused, blew the hair off her forehead with a puff, and put down a large bowl of mashed potatoes. "Roses are my most favorite of all flowers. And, every time I see this table, hauled by wagon all the way from Virginia, I just have to smile."

"To say nothing of your fine China and silver," Sarah commented.

"Yes. That too." Ellen paused a moment, savoring the scene, then called out, "E. B., bring in the roast, would you please? Eliza, call your Uncle John and the others to dinner. That's a girl."

The family trooped in, and finally the hubbub of aunts, uncles, cousins and siblings getting seated, subsided.

"Lord, bless this food," Uncle Alfred prayed, "and bless this family to use these, your gifts, to your glory, this day, and every day. Amen."

"Amen," rang around the table. Aunt Jane's long, "*A-a-a-men*!" lingered as an enthusiastic echo. Everyone smiled...

❊ ❊ ❊

At the end of the Indian Mission service everyone stood to sing.

O who will come and go with me,
I am bound for the Promised Land.

Edward's voice rang out loud and clear. He might feel nostalgic for the family in Indiana, but right now there was no place he'd rather be.

After dinner, the Indians offered to demonstrate their prowess in riding and shooting with bows and arrows, if the pioneers paid ten cents. Several wagons put in a penny each to watch the show.

"Did you see that?" Edward shouted as a young brave dropped off his pony and jumped back on, all the while the horse was galloping across the ground.

"William, do something!" Nancy Kelsey demanded as an Indian pranced by acting like a pony, young Caleb laughing and shouting, sitting on his shoulders hanging on to the Indian's long, black hair.

Shaking his head and shrugging, William watched his son and smiled. "Don't worry, darlin'. Indians love children."

"But what if he decides to *keep* our son?"

William patted her hand. "I don't think there's much chance of that." His glance took in the seventy or more men in the wagon party who were watching.

By the end of the show, Caleb and Lucy were running in circles, shouting and chasing each other. Soon, Ellen and redheaded George had joined in. As the older children quickly outdistanced him, Caleb began to pout.

Without thinking twice, Edward swooped the boy up, and together they surged in front.

"Me, me!" cried Lucy. Lewis settled her on his shoulders and joined in the race.

Several young Indians joined in as the others turned to run back to the starting line. The Indians easily beat the pioneers, but no one cared.

Sitting on the grass, gulping in great gasps of air, Edward realized how much he enjoyed being part of this traveling group. He felt every bit as comfortable, here on the limitless prairie, traveling with these friends, as he'd ever felt in Greencastle.

He could hardly wait to see what tomorrow would bring.

Chapter Seven

Later that evening, the men from their six-wagon group were sitting around the fire, discussing what the morrow would likely bring.

"I 'speck we'll need to elect a captain," William Kelsey said. His wife, Nancy was settling Lucy and Caleb for sleep in their tent next to the first wagon.

Edward turned to his cousin, Richard. "Would you like to be captain?"

Richard smiled. His eyes sparkled in the flickering light. Then, after a pause, he shook his head. "Thank you for asking. But no, I'd rather Gould was captain."

"I'll second that!" said Samuel Wilson. His son, George looked pleased his father had taken part in the discussion.

"Would you be willing?" asked Edward.

For a long moment, Gould didn't respond. They all sat in silence, except for the snapping of the logs on the fire.

Finally he said, "I'd be right proud to be considered your leader. Though, the other wagons might already be discussing members from their own groups.

"Seems to me the lot who arrived the day before we got here, have been getting acquainted. I wouldn't object to following their choice for captain."

"Maybe you could be second in command," offered Kelsey.

Gould nodded his head. "That'd be fine. We'll need to all work together. Every wagon cooperating. Not competing. Not jostling to get ahead. And be patient..."

Edward thought Gould looked particularly at Lewis, but it was hard to tell in the uncertain light.

"Remember," Gould continued, "the reason we need to form into a wagon train at all, is because from here on in the Indians will be getting less and less civilized. They catch one or two wagons all by their lonesome—too far ahead or straggling behind—they'll kill or wound the livestock, steal what they can, and leave the whites helpless at best. Kidnapped, or dead at worst."

Edward felt his heart pound. Everyone seemed just as affected at the picture Gould had painted. No one said a word.

"Added to that," Gould picked up where he'd left off, "it'll take every man—and woman, too—working as a team, to get our wagons and livestock across the rivers. We need a good captain, and willing members to all get where we're going."

***

Early the next morning, people from all of the wagons camped at the Mission met together to elect a leader. After some discussion, Jonas Sylvester, who had led a group of eight wagons from Pennsylvania, was chosen captain.

"He's quiet-spoken," Richard commented to Edward, "but decisive. I think he'll make a good leader."

Edward agreed, though he still favored Gould, who had accepted the position of second in command.

The first thing Sylvester did was have the wagons line up in the order they would travel, interspersing couples and families with children among wagons with only males. "This way we can easily aid and protect the females and children, if necessary," he explained.

"That seems reasonable," Richard commented.

"I'm glad our six are already set up that way," answered Lewis. "We can just remain as we've been all along."

It took quite a while, after the oxen were hitched to the wagons, for them to maneuver into one continuous line.

Sylvester assigned Gould to lead his group of six wagons in the middle of the sixty-wagon train.

"Now, we're going to put our wagons into a circle," Sylvester announced.

"Gould, you lead the last half of the train up alongside of the first half until we're traveling forward in pairs. When the two lines match up, you and I'll turn our wagon sideways across the trail. Then, each line of wagons spread out sideways to enclose a circular central area as a corral for the animals. This way they'll be easily protected if Indians threaten."

With hard work and practice, by that evening, the entire train could form a corral in only five minutes.

Before they broke up for supper, Sylvester established a rotation of sentinels to stay awake during a portion of each night, to guard the wagons and grazing animals from infiltration by Indians.

"No guns capped or cocked inside the encampment," Sylvester admonished. "If we don't allow the Indians inside, the only things you'll shoot will be your own dumb feet, or a precious wife or child. Am I clear on that?"

The men all nodded and shouted, "Yes!"

"Tomorrow, we start for Fort Kearny," he announced. "With luck, it should take about a week. Start your cattle to feed by three o'clock. Roll out by four.

"We'll travel till the sun gets high, then camp, cook, and eat till the heat is over. Then we'll start again and go till nearly dark." He looked around, grinned, and thrust his fist into the air.

"Hip, hip, hurray!" Shouts rang out. Hats flew into the air.

Edward and Lewis grinned and cheered, slapping each other silly. "We're on our way!"

Chapter Eight

Edward urged the Ashley's oxen forward. Grunted as a wheel landed, hard, in a depression in the track. He smiled as he watched William—taking a break from driving the wagon—and Nancy, walking hand in hand. Not much older than he, they were so obviously in love.

How could she, he wondered, be willing to set out for California, in her condition? To give birth along some empty wagon trail? No mid-wife? No family to help?

He was glad not to be responsible for a pregnant wife.

The thought brought Susanna to mind. Funny, he hadn't even thought about her until now...

⁂

Saturday, late August 1848

Edward whistled as he dressed. He'd had his weekly bath in the big tin tub in the kitchen. Now, donning his Sunday-go-to-meeting clothes, he looked forward with pleasant anticipation to having supper with Susanna and her family.

They'd been childhood friends. And, now... we're still friends, he thought, but no longer children.

He adjusted his tie, stopped whistling, called "goodbye" to his mother in the kitchen, and began walking to Susanna's house.

***

They ate supper at a table on the back stoop. The kitchen was still too hot, even though the meal had been cooked earlier, and was served cold.

"How would you get to California?" Susanna's eleven-year-old brother Tommy asked.

By now, the discovery of gold in California had moved to the front page of nearly every newspaper in the world. It had become a topic of conversation in every home in America. A topic that fascinated Edward.

"Well, I know you could sail from Boston, New York, or Chesapeake Bay. Even New Orleans, I guess. But you'd have to go all the way down Mexico and South America. Then nearly to the South Pole before you started up the other side." Edward shuddered. "I can't imagine bobbing around in a wooden ship, knowing all that cold dark water was underneath it!

"So, if I were to go, I'd go overland, I guess. Take a big wagon pulled by a team of oxen all the way across the prairie."

Tommy's eyes grew large. "Do you think you might do it? Go to California?"

"I've thought about it. But I don't know enough yet. Where to find water for the animals. How to cross the rivers. How best to go over the mountains guarding California from the rest of the United States.

"And, my folks said they would disown me if I dropped out of school before I graduated."

"But when you do... find out, I mean, and graduate, will you go?"

Edward responded with a shrug and quizzical half-smile, "I don't know. Maybe."

"Now don't be a pest," Mr. Collins admonished. "Eat your supper."

"More corn, Edward?" asked Mrs. Collins.

"Yes, please. And perhaps another slice of your delicious ham?"

"Of course."

"But, what if you went all that way, and there wasn't any gold left?" Tommy asked.

Perhaps because the others wondered the same thing, no one reprimanded him.

Edward swallowed. He thought for a moment. "Well, I'd probably turn around and come home again. But at least I'd have seen the elephant."

"There's *elephants* in California?" Tommy looked perplexed, while the others simply smiled.

"Haven't you ever heard that story?" Mr. Collins asked his son.

When Tommy shook his head, Mr. Collins began. "One day, when the circus was coming to a town for the first time, the poster said they had an elephant. Now, a farmer wanted to see this marvelous animal and, loading his wagon with produce to sell, set out for town.

"He arrived just in time to see the circus parade, headed by the promised elephant. The farmer was overjoyed to see such a huge and amazing beast. But, the farmer's horse was terrified and bolted, running all the way back to the farm.

"The next week, someone in town commiserated with the farmer because all he'd seen was the parade, and not the circus performance in the big tent.

"The farmer shook his head. 'It don't make no matter,' he said. 'I have seen the elephant.'"

* * *

After dinner, Edward and Susanna sat in the swing on the front porch. He pushed with his toe, making the swing move gently back and forth. The slight breeze felt refreshing as the evening cooled slightly.

Susanna's blue frock, and the ribbon tying her blond hair at the nape of her neck, exactly matched the blue of her eyes. Edward had a sudden urge to kiss her. He took a deep breath. I'm too old, he thought, for a kiss to be innocent. I'd want to hold her close. Be tempted to do more than that. But I don't even want to think about marriage, and a house, and babies.

He sighed and took her hand instead.

"I can't even imagine leaving Greencastle, and going all that way," she commented, her voice soft and dreamy. "I'd miss my family. Our house. The people I know. Places I'm used to."

"I know," Edward replied. "Sometimes, I feel that way, too. But, just the same, I'd love to see the elephant." Edward sat, quietly pushing the swing. Thinking.

"At the University, my favorite classes are in the history department. I love reading about great events, imagining what the people were thinking. Feeling. What it would be like to be caught up in the middle of it all.

"And now, *we're* in the middle of a great event. People are coming from all over the world—Europe, China—and all *I'd* have to do is cross the continent to California."

"But just that," Susanna shuddered, "would be a dreadfully hard and dangerous undertaking."

"True. But how would I feel, years from now—reading accounts of going to California, finding gold—knowing I could have done that, myself. I wouldn't have to imagine what people were feeling. I would know, first hand, what it's like to hold those shiny nuggets in my own hands!"

Susanna said nothing...

❊ ❊ ❊

Now, as Edward urged the Ashley's oxen on, he knew Susanna could not have done what Nancy was doing. Her silence had spoken volumes.

If she had begged him to stay in Greencastle, finish school, marry, and settle down, would he have agreed?

Looking around at the long string of wagons winding its way across the prairie, he felt relief that Susanna hadn't asked.

Chapter Nine

The next day, clouds covered the sky. Edward sniffed. He could smell rain in the air. Soon it was pouring down. Their wagon wheels barely turned, mired in mud. Walking next to the wagon, with Richard driving, Edward's boots sank into the muck. Each step made a sucking sound as he pulled a foot free and set it down again, one step closer to California.

At their mid-day stop, while the rain continued to fall, he cooked dinner on their sheet iron stove with its pipe stuck through the hole in the tent.

"This stove and tent were two really good purchases we made in St. Jo," he said as he stirred some maple syrup into a pot of beans. His mother, once she'd accepted the fact he was going to California despite her protests, had taught him to cook the basics—biscuits, coffee—and beans. Beans with maple syrup. Beans with ham. Beans with bacon.

"Yup," Richard agreed. Just then Lewis entered the tent, slapping his hat against his knee, dislodging a shower of raindrops. "The oxen are happily eating prairie grass," he reported. "Don't even seem to care that they're standing hock-deep in mud and the rain is still coming down."

After the mid-day dinner, they packed up. Started forward. This time, Edward sat on their wagon seat. The rain had slackened to a mere drizzle. The mud, however, was no less tenacious as it grabbed at hooves, boots, and wheels.

Shortly after starting out, Edward spotted a chest of drawers by the trail. Someone had to lighten their load because their mules or oxen couldn't pull the wagon through the mud.

Pointing to the chest, Edward called down to Richard, who was walking beside the wagon, "Aren't we glad we bought strong oxen?"

"Yes! But, why would anyone bring something as heavy—and unnecessary—as a chest of drawers?" Richard responded.

They both shrugged their shoulders and shook their heads.

* * *

Two nights later, Edward was awakened by loud, shrieking sobs coming from another wagon. By the time he'd stuck his feet in boots, lit the lantern, and grabbed his gun, his tent mates had joined him.

The sounds were coming from the Kelsey's tent. Edward was the first to reach the flap. Hair disheveled, tears streaming down a face grotesque in grief, Nancy rocked her son in her arms. Caleb had been throwing up; vomit covered both himself and his mother. If that weren't enough, the stench of loose bowels made breathing difficult. But now, there was a terrible stillness to the boy.

Cholera! Barely able to hold down his own nausea, Edward called out, "William, take little Lucy to the river and wash yourselves and all your clothing!"

When William didn't move, Edward shouted, "Do it, man! Now!"

Gould arrived as William, with his daughter still wrapped in her blanket, stumbled out of the tent.

Kneeling down, Gould said, "Nancy. Hush now, Nancy." He reached out. Touched her arm. "He's gone, dear. See? He's no longer vomiting. You need to go wash yourself. Let us bury your boy."

"No-o-o," she sobbed, clutching her son.

Gently, Gould pried her fingers open. Took the now still bundle of child and excrement from her hands.

"Go now, woman. You can't help him any more. Go to your husband and daughter. Wash up. We'll take care of this."

Gould turned to his wife, who stood on the edge of the onlookers. "Go with her. Just don't touch her. Or her clothing."

Edward said, "I'll see if I can find clothing or blankets in their wagon. Mrs. Gould can take it to them to put on when they get out of the river."

He remembered his father telling the family about cholera when that dread disease broke out in St. Louis in early 1849. Thinking about it made him shake his head in despair…

"You have no idea how dangerous cholera is," Father had said. "There's no cure. And it's a horrible way to die. You vomit over and over. Even after you have nothing left in your stomach. *And* you have uncontrollable diarrhea—both at the same time. Extreme cramps and pain. Believe me, you don't want to be anywhere close to where cholera is, if you can help it."

And, because his father was a pharmacist, and knew what he was talking about, Edward believed.

❊❊❊

The sun was rising as Edward and Richard finished tamping down the soil on the tiny grave. The members of their six-wagon family comforted the bereaved parents as best they could, while the rest of the wagon train stood respectfully by.

Edward tried to replace his last image of small Caleb with the better memory of their time at the Sac Mission. Recalled him laughing, hanging on to the Indian's hair as the man pranced like a pony. Remembered the feel of the small boy's squirming, excited body as they raced to catch up with the 'big kids.'

Tried to forget the stench that, even now, filled his nostrils. What he'd seen—and smelled—that awful night would be forever seared into his memory.

"As this is the Sabbath," Sylvester announced, "we will stay in camp today. We'll have worship service, and pay our respects at young Caleb's grave, as soon as breakfast and chores are done."

The members of the six-wagon family surrounded a stoic William and softly weeping Nancy by the small patch of freshly turned earth. Many from the large wagon train gathered around the area.

"Mama, why did those men throw Caleb away?" Lucy's childish voice broke the silence. "Was he naughty?"

"No. Of course not. Caleb was a good little boy." Nancy knelt down. Straightened Lucy's bonnet. Gave her a hug. "God needed a good little boy to go to heaven. To play among the stars with Jesus and the angels."

Edward heard a muttering of voices behind him.

"He may have been a good little boy," a man from the large group of onlookers murmured. "But, somebody sinned. Most likely his father or mother."

"Why do you say that?" another voice asked.

"Read the Bible, man! It's all over the Old Testament. God punished sinners by bringing on plagues or other disasters. Someone had to sin for this to happen."

Edward prayed neither William nor Nancy could hear the talk. Debated turning to shush them.

"But, if he needed to go to heaven," Lucy persisted, "why did they bury him in the ground?"

"Because, Caleb had to die first. It's sort of like going to sleep, but when he wakes up he'll be in heaven."

Nancy hugged Lucy. "Since Caleb is sleeping now, why don't you say your bedtime prayer?"

The little girl knelt by the grave, her chubby fingers folded in prayer.

"Now I lay me down to sleep..."

Even the slightest rustling of people hushed as they listened.

"I pray the Lord my soul to keep.

If I should die before I wake,

I pray the Lord my soul to take."

Edward looked around. His weren't the only cheeks damp with tears.

For what seemed a long time, the only sound was the soft movement of a breeze through the grasses and trees, and the twittering of birds.

Shall we gather at the river,

A lone soprano voice sang, soft but clear.

Where bright angel feet have trod

Two or three women joined in.

With its crystal tide forever
Flowing by the throne of God.

By now, everyone had begun singing the comforting, familiar hymn.

Yes we'll gather at the river,
The beautiful, the beautiful, river,
Gather with the saints at the river,
That flows by the throne of God.

* * *

During the dinner break, two days later, Gould suddenly bolted from the cluster of wagons and dashed to the trees and bushes growing along the river they were planning to cross that afternoon.

Mrs. Gould ran after him calling, "Husband! Husband! What's the matter?"

Chapter Ten

Edward and Lewis quickly overtook and outdistanced Mrs. Gould. Running, panting to the trees, they saw Gould vomiting everything he had just eaten.

"Go away!" he shouted. "It's the cholera! Don't come any closer."

Just then, the uncontrollable diarrhea, common to the dread disease, began.

Mrs. Gould arrived and started toward her husband. Edward grabbed her arm, as Gould reiterated, "It's the cholera."

"You really shouldn't touch him," Edward said, gently.

"But, but..."

"Nothing you can do," Gould gasped, wincing.

"Is that true?" the distraught woman asked.

Edward sighed. "Yes. It's true. My father's a pharmacist. And he told me there is no cure. No treatment."

She sank to her knees and began to cry.

Just then, young Ellen arrived. Mother and daughter wept in each other's arms.

Sylvester, and others from the wagon train, drawn by the commotion, began gathering a few feet from where Gould lay, retching and moaning.

After a hurried consultation, Sylvester declared, "There's no reason for the entire wagon train to delay here. In fact, it's better that we separate ourselves from the cholera. We will leave, cross the river, and continue our journey as soon as everyone is packed and ready to go.

"However," he continued, "I would ask a couple of you to volunteer to remain. Help Mrs. Gould and Ellen. Prepare a grave for Mr. Gould."

Edward hesitated. No one knew, for sure, what caused cholera. By staying and helping, would he be endangering his own life?

He looked at Gould, whom he admired above all others on the wagon train. Gazed at his wife and young daughter, nearly the same age as his brother.

"I'll stay," he called out, before he had a chance to change his mind.

"The three of us will help," Richard agreed, without even consulting Lewis.

"My brother and I will give a hand," said Benjamin, to his younger brother's nod of approval.

"My boy and I will stay," offered Samuel Wilson, in response to his son's look of hero-worship. Whatever John Cummings was doing, George wanted to do it with him.

"Gould probably wouldn't have gotten cholera, if he hadn't helped with Caleb. Least I can do is offer help," said William Kelsey.

"My Frank will help, too," Mary Ann said, with a lift of her chin and an adoring smile for her husband.

"But, sweetheart, you—"

"Mary Ann," Mrs. Gould interrupted. "Consider your condition."

Mary Ann held her hands protectively around her stomach. "Oh, I'll keep my distance. I wouldn't want anything to happen to the baby. But, I don't want to move on without you.

"You're the closest thing I have to a mother now, and I won't risk going into labor without you to help me."

And so it was decided the six-wagon group of families would remain behind to render whatever assistance they could.

By the next day, Gould was retching a violent discharge of whitish, yellowish matter.

"Water," he cried feebly. "Water..."

Edward carefully handed him a cup of water and a few grains of dried opium for the pain.

On the third day, while Gould was still alive, the men began digging a grave.

"It seems unfeeling to dig his grave so close to where he's lying," Richard commented, quietly.

"If he's aware of anything, he knows we have to dig it here—and now," Edward answered.

"Although Gould is slender," Richard said, "he is tall. The hole will have to be long."

It didn't take long before Edward had to stop shoveling and wiped the sweat from his face. His shirt stuck to his sopping-wet body. The hot, moist air made it seem impossible to breathe. Stars began to dance in front of his eyes.

"Here E.B., have some water." Lewis put a cup in Edward's outstretched hand.

"Thanks." Edward gulped the water. "I'm glad we're all in this together."

He handed the empty cup back, and gritting his teeth, began to dig the hard-pack ground again.

By the next day, Gould was screaming in agony from cramps in his legs and body. And then his body turned blue. Opium no longer relieved his pain...

* * *

Doing the best they could to keep from getting the excrement on themselves, the men used shovels to gently roll and prod Gould's body into the grave. Although he was thoroughly dead, his body was strangely warm and continued to twitch.

They also buried as much excrement as possible in Gould's grave with him. Then they covered the whole cavity with sweet-smelling soil.

"Remember what Ware's book said," Edward reminded them when they finished. "We need to wash everything. Probably even before reading the Bible and praying over his grave."

They washed the shovels in the river first. Meanwhile Mrs. Gould and Nancy gathered clean clothes for the men and laid them on the grassy bank.

After washing their clothes and boots, Edward and the others began cleansing their bodies.

"Ahhh," he sighed, as the cooling, moving water washed over his hot, sweaty body. "This feels like a baptism."

"Poor Gould," said Richard, floating next to him. "Please God, let no one else get cholera."

"I can't believe a good man like Gould was struck down for his sin by God's wrath," said Lewis.

"Or that Caleb's parents were such sinners that a sweet child should be sacrificed for their wrongs," agreed Edward. "I just can't."

He closed his eyes, letting the cool water cleanse him. Trying to let it erase the horrible stench of death by cholera.

Softly, he began singing, without thought or will...

Shall we gather at the river...

Chapter Eleven

“I don’t care what those men from the wagon train said, my husband was a good man.” Gould’s widow and Edward were enjoying a last cup of coffee before retiring.

“Just look how he took me and Ellen in after her daddy died.”

“You mean, Gould isn’t… wasn’t her father?”

“Oh no. My first husband was her father. Her name’s Ellen Frances Logan.”

“I wasn’t aware of that,” Edward said. “But, I agree with you, I always felt Gould was an excellent man. I can’t believe either his death, or Caleb’s, was the result of God’s wrath over sinful living.”

A companionable silence stretched out between them.

“There we were,” Mrs. Gould mused, “a young widow and a three-year-old girl. And Mr. Gould, whose wife and baby had recently died. It just made good sense.

“Oh, he wasn’t the heart-stopping love of my life. *That* was Ellen’s daddy… Lord, Lord, I couldn’t go through losing the likes of him more than once in a lifetime. But Mr. Gould treated us both with respect. Courtesy. Gentleness.” She sighed.

Edward didn't know what to say, so he quietly patted her hand.

"I'm worried about Ellen, though," Gould's widow broke the silence. "He was as much a father as she can remember."

"What will you do now?"

"Oh, we'll keep on going, I guess. To California. We have nothing to go back to, even if we could find a party traveling east to take us in."

Edward gazed at Mrs. Gould. The flames of the fire played light and shadows on her face. Whether it was the physical activity of walking the better part of fifteen miles a day, or the loss of a good man she admired, if not loved, she seemed thinner. Less robust. She now exuded a gritty determination. He had no doubt she'd make it to California, somehow.

"We'll be happy to have you and Ellen with us on the trip to California, Missus Gould."

"Please. After all we've been through, you can call me Caroline."

"We'll be happy to have you with us... Caroline."

* * *

The next day, the six wagons left for Fort Kearny. That they were leaving two bodies, buried on the prairie just one week apart, weighed heavily on them all.

"Why don't you come ride with me," Edward invited Ellen who was trudging, chin on chest, beside the wagon he was driving.

She looked up, made an attempt at a lopsided smile.

"Whoa, there." He stopped the oxen long enough for her to scramble up. Then, with a cluck and a slap of the reins, urged them on again.

"I'm sorry about your father's death," he offered.

"He wasn't my father."

"I know. But he was a father to you, anyway."

She sniffed and nodded.

"And you'll miss him."

Another nod of the bonnet.

"Are you worried, or just sad?" he asked gently.

After a pause she looked up. "Both, I guess."

"What worries you the most?"

"That my mother will die and leave me alone."

Edward put his arm around the young girl's shoulders. "Look around you," he told her. "What do you see?"

"Grasses. Trees and bushes."

"Are you alone on the grasses?"

"No."

"And if, just if, your mother wasn't here, would you be alone?"

"I guess not."

"You guessed correctly. You've got a whole family here. Some of us are like older brothers. Some are like aunts and uncles. You've got a little cousin, Lucy, and another baby coming soon.

"You've got a big family who loves you, and would never leave you orphaned."

Ellen sat straighter and gave Edward a real smile.

He had a thought.

"Now," he continued, "there's something I want you to do for me. For our whole extended family, actually."

She gave him a questioning look.

"See little Lucy, there?"

She nodded.

"She misses her little brother. She's afraid, too, because she doesn't understand what dying is. Could you, just for a part of each day, walk with her? Hold her hand? Play tag, like she and Caleb used to do? Help her pick some flowers to give her mother, who is missing her little boy, too?"

Ellen nodded, her face serious. "I can do that."

"I thought you could." Edward smiled. "Are you ready to get down now?"

Edward felt a wave of tenderness as Ellen got off the wagon, walked to Lucy, and took her hand.

Chapter Twelve

For the better part of two days, the six wagons traveled toward Fort Kearny without incident.

Then, toward evening of that second day, Mary Ann Ashley stopped walking. Held her stomach. Then continued on. A few minutes later, she stopped again.

"Darlin' what's the matter?" Frank called out.

"Probably nothing. Just a touch of indigestion, I guess."

But, a little while later, she stopped. Sat on the ground and moaned.

Caroline Gould stopped her wagon and rushed to Mary Ann's side. "Where does it hurt?"

"H...here. Ooooh..." she moaned.

"You just hold on," Caroline told her.

"Edward, we need to stop now. Here. Mary Ann's about to have her baby!"

In no time at all, the wagons formed a circle. Caroline Gould directed the men to empty the Ashley's wagon enough to make room for a bed to be made up on the floor for Mary Ann. Then she and Nancy clambered in to help.

"Make a fire," Caroline ordered. "Bring buckets of water. Then leave us alone while you get to your own suppers."

To the accompaniment of moans, encouraging murmurs, and occasional heart-rending shrieks, the men set up camp, watched their livestock as they grazed, and put together a cold supper. Frank turned white, stopped moving, stopped breathing, every time he heard his wife cry out in pain.

After a long night, during which no one got any sleep, they were rewarded with a baby's lusty cry.

"Congratulations, Ashley!" the men shouted. "You're a father!"

The sun was casting shadows when Caroline called out, "Frank, come on in here. Meet your new son!"

"It's a boy!" everyone exclaimed.

"What's his name?"

When Frank came out, he held the tiny, red-faced baby in his arms. "This is Joshua Caleb Ashley," he announced. Turning to William with a solemn look, he said, "The Caleb is for your son."

William, tears in his eyes, walked over. Touched the tiny cheek with a work-hardened finger. Smiled and whispered, "Welcome to the world little Joshua Caleb Ashley."

Ellen danced up on tiptoes to see the baby. Touched his hand. "Oh, look! He's holding my finger!" Grinning from ear to ear, she declared, "I think he likes me."

Edward looked up in time to see Caroline beaming at her daughter. For the first time in over a week, the mother smiled, her blue eyes twinkling, a dimple gracing her cheek.

Nancy emerged from the wagon and walked to her husband's arms. Tears streamed down her cheeks, but she smiled. "Two deaths, and then life. We have cause to feel hope." William kissed her while everyone nodded.

* * *

Edward awoke about noon, feeling grungy and headachy from sleeping during the day. He got to work bringing a pot of beans that had been soaking for a couple of days to a boil, adding molasses and bacon for flavor.

He thought nothing of it when he noticed the Cummings brothers talking quietly with Wilson and his son, George.

After they'd eaten their dinners, they beckoned Edward, Richard and Lewis to the area outside the ring of wagons.

"It didn't matter we stopped to bury little Caleb," said Ben. "It was Sunday anyways."

"And we stayed to help with Gould," his brother, John added with a touch of self-righteousness. "Even though it *did* take four days for him to die, and another to bury him."

"And we lost another day with Mary Ann having her baby and all," added Sam Wilson. His son George was watching the conversation as if he were following a sporting event—his head turning first this way, then that.

"But now the baby's here, the whole wagon train will move at a snail's pace—" John started.

"—Mary Ann can't possibly cover anywhere near fifteen miles a day," Ben interrupted.

"So, we propose those of us who don't have children to slow us down," Sam concluded, "take off after dinner here and make tracks for Fort Kearny as fast as we can."

"You mean, just leave Caroline, the Ashley's, and Kelsey's on their own?" asked Richard.

"We can't do that!" Edward agreed. The idea made him feel a bit sick.

"At one time I'd have thought you were right," Lewis interjected. "Losing time, while others are going to get to California and all that gold ahead of us—"

"You can't help cholera," Ben interrupted, while his brother nodded in agreement. "But it was plain idiocy for Mary Ann to take off across the country when she was in a family way."

"We can't just leave them without any defenses in Indian country," Edward exclaimed. "How much will you enjoy your gold, knowing you left women and children without proper guardians?"

"They've got two men, and I bet Missus Gould can shoulder a gun almost as good as a man, if she has to."

"You have no idea what Indians can do," Edward commented. "My grandfather, Leroy Daingerfield, told stories from his older brother, William, who fought in the French and Indian War.

"In that war, if Indians captured English settlers, they marched them to their camps," Edward continued. "Once there, the prisoners had to watch in horror as their fellow white men were tied to posts, and fires built, far enough away to slowly roast them alive. It took a long, long time for them to die. All the while, the other prisoners had to watch, knowing this would be their fate as well."

"That was a hundred years ago!" Benjamin exclaimed, after a moment's stunned silence. "They don't do those things now. Ware doesn't say anything like that in his book.

He just says to guard your camps to keep them from stealing your stock."

"Well, you can take off as fast as you want, but I'm going to stay with the others," said Edward.

"Why?" asked Ben.

"Because I promised Ellen."

"What did you promise her?" asked Sam Wilson.

"That we wouldn't leave her. Remember," Edward said, "it's only been four days since she lost her daddy. She's terrified if her mother dies, she'll be left alone in the middle of the endless prairie. I told her she had a family in these six wagons. That we wouldn't leave her orphan."

Edward looked from face to face. No one said anything. Or met his eyes.

He turned, and started to walk back to camp.

"Wait up," called Richard. "We'll stay together. The three of us."

"Yeah, we'll stay," Lewis chimed.

"The three of you are plenty of men for four wagons," Benjamin said. "We'll go on ahead."

* * *

The two wagons rolled away before the others had loaded up after the dinner break. Edward watched them with a sense of foreboding. And disappointment. He couldn't imagine what the others were feeling. Especially little Ellen.

They made slow progress toward Fort Kearny. Mary Ann trudged on, clutching her baby. If one of the men relieved Caroline Gould of driving, she walked beside Mary Ann and carried the tiny mite.

But every couple of hours, Mary Ann had to stop to nurse her son. The oxen enjoyed the extra time to rest and feed.

Lewis would catch Edward's eye, and with a raised eyebrow, remind him they were falling farther behind. That spring and summer wouldn't last forever. That snow would begin to fall in the High Sierras long before fall even started, lower down.

They traveled right through the Sabbath, figuring they'd rested enough along the way.

"I will lift up mine eyes unto the hills," Edward murmured as he drove the oxen, "from whence cometh my help. My help cometh from the Lord which made heaven and earth." Edward's eyes took in the expanse of prairie. The blue sky dotted with puffs of white clouds.

"Please God," he prayed, "be with us. Give us traveling mercies. Let no more die."

Toward noon of the next day, the four wagons topped a slight swell in the prairie, and looked down to see—Indians! Not just a small hunting party, but a whole encampment. At least fifty. Maybe more.

Stunned, the small party—five men, three women, two children, and a newborn babe—came to a stop. No place to hide!

Chapter Thirteen

"What do we do now?" asked Lewis in a whisper.

Edward, his heart thumping, swallowed. "I have no idea."

"We don't have enough wagons or men to make a defensive circle," Richard said, stating the obvious. "And nowhere near enough to corral all the livestock."

"Oh-oh, they've spotted us!" Lewis reached inside the wagon for his gun.

By now the others had joined them.

Edward put a restraining hand on Lewis' arm. "Don't be daft, man! Put that away!"

"Pulling a gun will, for sure, get us killed or captured," William Kelsey hissed.

A delegation of five Indians had jumped on ponies and now approached.

Caroline Gould squinted, looking at the encampment. "They've got women and children there. I can't imagine they want a fight, even though we're easily out-numbered."

The Indians stopped a short distance from the wagons, and one gravely raised a hand in a sign of peace.

The group by the wagons looked to Richard, who equally solemnly raised his right hand, palm out.

The Indians rode slowly forward. Still mounted, their leader said, “You trade?”

Edward looked at the others, who all shrugged their shoulders. Again, they looked to Richard for leadership.

“Uh, I guess so.” He nodded in agreement to the Indians, and then asked, “What do you have?”

One of the braves came forward, proudly exhibiting a bulky leather pouch. Inside were four large chunks of freshly dressed, boneless meat.

At the sight, Edward could taste the succulent meat. He could actually smell the scent of it roasting over a fire. After nearly three weeks of eating nothing but variations on boiled beans three times a day, he would have traded almost anything for that meat.

“What do you suppose it is?” asked Lewis.

“I don’t know,” responded William. “Deer, antelope…?”

“Or buffalo!” Frank Ashley grinned, his eyes gleaming.

“How much?” Richard asked the first Indian.

“You have fire stick?”

“He means a gun,” Edward said quietly.

“No.” Richard said firmly shaking his head. “We’ll *not* trade a fire stick,”

“I’d love to have fresh meat,” Lewis said, “but not at the price of a gun!”

“Besides,” added William, “do we really want to be responsible for giving more guns to Indians?”

“Not only is the gun too high a price to pay,” said Edward, with a feeling of regret, “but, that’s more meat than we can eat. I'd love to have it all, but we can't smoke, salt, or dry it. And, there's only so much we can eat before it spoils."

Richard pointed to two of the roasts. "Two meat," he said, holding up two fingers. "One knife." He held up one finger and pointed to the hunting knife in the scabbard on his belt.

The lead brave held up two fingers. "Two meat." He held up four fingers. "Four knife."

Pointing, Richard said, "Two meat." Then, holding up two fingers, "two knives."

The five braves held a serious discussion, and finally held out the two roasts.

Holding out his hand, Richard said, "Edward, give me your knife."

Meanwhile, Mary Ann Ashley stood holding baby Joshua. Caroline Gould, Ellen by her side, and Nancy Kelsey with Lucy holding tightly to her skirt, stood close by. Mary Ann watched as other Indians wandered over.

A young squaw walked up to her and smiled. Mary Ann's heart seemed to beat double-time.

"Indians love babies," she whispered to Caroline. "They've been known to steal them." She clutched her baby so tightly he started to cry.

"Shhh," she cooed, loosening her grip.

The squaw touched baby Joshua's arm, then pointed to a baby tied to her own back.

Mary Ann peered and exclaimed, "Look, Nancy, how snug her baby is!"

The Indian took Mary Ann's hand and gestured toward the encampment.

Mary Ann turned to Caroline. "Do I dare go with her?"

Caroline looked the young woman up and down. "I guess it'd be alright."

"Come with me? I'm afraid to go by myself." She handed Joshua to Nancy.

Caroline knelt to look young Ellen in the eye. "Will you go with us? See what the Indian lady wants? And maybe keep your eyes open, ready to run back to the wagons for help, if we see the need?"

Young Ellen's eyes shone. "Yes, mamma! I surely would like to do that."

Mary Ann, Caroline, and Ellen entered the encampment, wide-eyed with wonder as they took in the sight of several teepees made of buffalo hides, sewn together and laid over frames of poles. Children ran, playing tag in and out among the teepees, while dogs lay in the shade, and women sat on rugs visiting as they scraped the fat and flesh from hides.

"Look, mamma!" Ellen cried out, pointing. "Isn't that the cutest little puppy?"

Caroline nodded agreement, without letting go of Ellen's hand.

Meanwhile, the squaw had disappeared into a teepee. She soon emerged with an empty cradleboard in her hand.

Standing in front of Mary Ann, she thrust the object into her hands. "You..." the squaw grunted.

"Why, it's beautiful!" Mary Ann exclaimed, taking in the intricate carving and painted decorations on the wooden frame. "Look, it's even got a sun shade over the head. And a darling feather and bead ornament dangling down where the baby can see it. It's the *dearest* thing I've ever seen!"

The squaw came back out with a handful of dried moss. She took Mary Ann's arm and pulled her to return to the wagons.

Once there, she showed Mary Ann how to lay baby Joshua on the cradleboard, making a nest of the moss, not only as a cushion, but also to absorb any moisture the baby might create. Then she wrapped the soft leather around him, tying the thongs securely.

"Papoose," she said, proudly.

Mary Ann took the squaw's hand. "Thank you! Thank you, so much."

She walked in a small circle, waving her arms in the air. "Look, I can walk with both hands free. And the baby doesn't feel anywhere near as heavy with his weight on my back."

She turned to Frank. "We've got to give her something nice in exchange for this wonderful gift."

"We brought beads and such to trade," he answered.

"This has to be something special! Not just some cheap old beads!" She set the baby in its cradleboard on the ground, leaning against the wagon wheel, and crawled in to look for something suitable.

Everything she found seemed too ordinary—or necessary for their own survival. Finally, she found the perfect gift. Held it to her breast. *Should I? Could I?*

"But darlin'," Frank exclaimed when she clambered down from the wagon. "Are you sure? That was your grandmother's mirror. It's a family treasure, and we don't have another one."

Mary Ann looked at the silver-framed hand-mirror. She remembered it sitting on her grandmother's dresser, a comb and brush on either side. "I know. But, I'm going to thank this woman every step of the way to California, for her gift to me."

She put the precious mirror into the Indian's hands. When the squaw saw her reflection, she jumped in fright, almost dropping the gift.

"She's never seen a mirror," Mary Ann whispered in astonishment.

Mary Ann took the woman's hand and guided the mirror to reflect both their faces, side by side.

When the squaw smiled in wonder, Mary Ann knew she'd picked the right thing. As the other Indians pressed around the squaw to see their own faces, she was even gladder she had chosen her grandmother's mirror as the gift.

Taking Mary Ann's hand, the Indian pressed it to her chest. To Mary Ann's delight she felt the thumping of the squaw's heart.

* * *

As the small wagon train started down the track toward Fort Kearny, Mary Ann said to Caroline, "Can you believe what just happened? We were so frightened of the Indians, and instead of harming us, they traded fresh meat for all of us, and gave me this wonderful papoose board."

"Who would have thought it," said Caroline with a smile that nearly matched Mary Ann's.

Chapter Fourteen

On Wednesday, May twenty-ninth, the four wagons reached the Platt River and Fort Kearny. Here the trail from St. Joseph and Independence, coming up from Missouri, met the trail coming down from Council Bluffs, Iowa.

It took a while, but they finally found space to unhitch their oxen amongst the large number of other wagons. They had been so vulnerable—just four wagons all by themselves—they welcomed joining the hustle and bustle of others migrating west. In vain, they looked around for any of their earlier wagon mates.

"They're likely long gone," Lewis said. Edward heard a tone of disappointment in his voice.

"If we had gone with them, we'd have missed the Indians, and the delicious fresh meat we've been eating," rejoined Edward.

Lewis' scowl switched to a grin. "You're right!" he exclaimed.

Fort Kearney, the first of several United States military posts they would come to on their way to California, was built primarily of blocks of sod instead of bricks. Edward noted only eight houses made of lumber, which, he was told, came overland from the far-away Missouri River.

At this point, the Platte River was about a mile wide, shallow, and filled with sandbars.

"The water looks disgusting," Ellen complained.

"Try putting a little of this alum in the pail," Edward suggested.

A short time later, Ellen exclaimed, "It works! All the clay sank to the bottom of the pail, and the water's clear." She looked at him in wonder. "How did you know to do that?"

"My father taught me," Edward answered. "He's the one who gave me the alum to bring with us."

They spent two days making repairs on the wagons, washing clothes, and buying fresh supplies. The canned fruit and fresh fish would be a welcome change in their diet. During this time, Edward wrote another piece for *The Argus.*

Describing the cholera deaths of young Caleb and Gould brought a lump to his throat. He hoped his writing would somehow be a fitting tribute for the laughing boy, and the man he'd looked up to as a mentor. Adding the birth of Joshua Caleb Ashley and his papoose board ended the article on a happier note.

Edward took the letter to the post headquarters where he saw it dropped into a mail pouch marked for St. Louis. From the fort, it would join the weekly mailbag on its way to St. Louis, Greencastle, and Indianapolis. He could only guess how long the mail might take. While not the nearly two months it had taken them, letters would certainly take over a month to reach Greencastle.

***

On Saturday, June first, their four wagons joined a forty-wagon train following the Platte River west. The large group from Council Bluffs gave them a friendly welcome. At the first mid-day stop, the train broke up into groups of six or seven wagons each. They shared campfires and food for dinner.

Edward was pleased when, after eating, Ellen brought a new friend she'd just met. "Mr. Daingerfield," she said with a big smile—a rare event since her father's death, "this is Hannah. She's in the wagon train from Council Bluffs, and she's going to walk with me this afternoon."

Edward shook Hannah's hand solemnly. "I'm very pleased to meet you, Hannah. And I'm even more glad that you're going to be Ellen's friend."

He was also happy to meet Hannah's father, Weston Clark, the wagon train captain.

"Where are you all from?" asked Clark, shaking hands with Edward, Richard, and Lewis. "And, what did you do there?"

"Greencastle, Indiana," answered Richard. "My cousin, Edward dropped out of Indiana Asbury University to go to California. He's our resident historian and newspaper columnist. And our friend Lewis is champing at the bit to get his hands on enough gold to buy a farm when he returns to Greencastle and marries his fiancé Elizabeth. As for me, I'm sort of along for the ride. No sweetheart at home. No farm to run. Mostly curious, I guess. What about you?"

"My wife, daughter, and I are from Cedar Rapids, Iowa. I left my brother and his wife to care for the family farm while we go see what this gold hullabaloo is all about. When we get back, they'll share half the profits of the farm with us, and we'll share half our gold with them. Hopefully, we'll all come out ahead."

Crossing the Platte River at Courthouse Rock a week later, they saw a few wagons camped a short distance from the river. A large hand-written sign *"CHOLERA"* propped against a rock, warned them of the danger.

Thankful for the warning, they established their camp some distance upstream from the wagons that had the dread disease. If there was anything they could have done to help, they would have, and gladly. But everyone knew nothing could be done.

"Please, God, not again," Edward prayed.

This time, his prayer was answered.

Edward continued to write in his journal as they traveled across the Nebraska Territory. *Saturday, June 8, Camp at Courthouse Rock. Rest on Sunday.*

A week later, nearing Wyoming, he wrote, *Saturday, June 15, Camp at Chimney Rock. It resembles a lookout tower on top of a mound of earth. Rest on Sunday.*

And, the next day: *One day's easy travel to Scotts Bluffs. In the distance it looks like a splendid old fort. I can imagine warriors streaming out, ready for battle.*

From the top of Scotts Bluffs we see the peaks of the Rocky Mountains.

On Friday, June twenty-first, they arrived at Fort Laramie.

Chapter Fifteen

They made camp on the banks of the Laramie River where it flowed into the South Platte. Here, grasses still grew, though sparsely, so the livestock could feed. Nearer the fort, somewhat over a mile above the fork, the earth had been grazed down to bare dirt.

"Mama," exclaimed Ellen. "What is *that?'* Her face was screwed up in a look of revulsion.

A short distance from shore, on the narrow sand bar of an island, stood a leafless tree. Silhouetted against the hard blue sky they saw the lifeless, nearly skeletal form of an Indian, hung like a crucifix, from its branches.

"That's the way the Plains Indians take care of their dead," Edward explained. "I read about it in one of the books I borrowed from the Asbury University library. They don't bury them in the ground, like we do. They leave them to dry out on a tree scaffold, with treasures on the ground at their feet, to accompany them into the afterlife."

❊ ❊ ❊

Weston Clark organized the men to take turns staying with the wagons, to discourage the woebegone Plains

Indians in their teepee villages surrounding the fort from helping themselves to everything from trinkets to oxen.

Edward, Richard, Caroline and Ellen, William, Nancy, and little Lucy, and several others, walked together on the hot, dusty, treeless way to the fort.

"Would you look at all that!" exclaimed Caroline, pointing to the litter of abandoned wagons, and surplus supplies.

"That's a perfectly good shovel," commented William.

"And clothes and shoes," said Nancy, shaking her head.

Seeing what the anxious pioneers had discarded, Edward felt the threat. "The Rocky Mountains, the desert of the Great Basin, and the barrier of the High Sierras lie between here and California. I guess people are beginning to lighten their loads."

"But, Fort Laramie is only a third of the way from the Missouri River to Sacramento," objected William Kelsey.

"Will we have *enough* supplies?" asked Nancy, anxiously. "Or are we taking *too much* for the oxen to pull?"

"The better question is, will we make it before snow falls in the Sierras?" William replied.

"You might as well ask, will we make it at all?" said Richard.

❊ ❊ ❊

Fort Laramie had a fascinating history. Back in 1834, fur traders built the original adobe fort, named Fort John. Lieutenant Daniel Woodbury of the Corps of Engineers purchased it on June 26, 1849 on the advice of Thomas Fitzpatrick.

A former mountain man called "Broken Hand" by the Indians, Fitzpatrick had become the first Agent for the Indians of the Upper Platte and Arkansas. His written report stated... "a post at or in the vicinity of Laramie is much wanted."

Fitzpatrick had argued, they'd need a large fort—three hundred mounted men a least—in the vicinity of the buffalo range where the most formidable Indian tribes were rapidly congregating... and game decreasing.

Some buildings had been constructed outside the adobe walls of the fort. "Look Lucy," Nancy said, pointing, "a real store!"

"I suspect it's the last one we'll see before we get to California," William said, smiling at his wife.

"Well, then, we'd best stock up here," she replied.

"Remember all the abandoned wagons and supplies we saw coming in," Caroline admonished. "Don't buy more than your oxen can pull over those mountains."

"What's that other building over there?" asked Ellen. "It looks nice with the veranda all around it."

"According to Ware's book, that must be the Post Headquarters and Bachelor Officers Quarters," said Edward.

❊ ❊ ❊

"Why there's a whole small town in here!" exclaimed Richard, as they entered the adobe walls of the fort proper. He looked around the hundred-and-thirty foot open square. It was framed with rooms, also built of adobe, and attached to the fifteen-foot high walls. Wooden palisades topped those fort walls.

On the open parade ground, a troop of uniformed soldiers marched in formation, following the shouted orders of their captain. A large American flag flew from a tall pole. Unconsciously, Caroline put her hand over her heart as she gazed at the red, white, and blue.

"It's like seeing a tiny piece of the United States out here in the Indian Territory," she said, almost reverently.

The two days the wagon train spent at Fort Laramie passed in a flurry of buying and trading for supplies to see them through the rest of the journey to the "Promised Land". This was a last chance to trade in worn-out, exhausted horses for sturdier mules and oxen.

"Aren't we glad we got *our* oxen in St. Joseph?" whispered Edward to Richard.

Members of the wagon train shopped for provisions of grain, flour, bread, and other staples from the Post Quartermaster. A sutler's store, outside the walls, supplied canned goods, liquor, patent medicines, lotions, muslin, and sunbonnets in exchange for coins and valuables.

The canned fruit and fresh fish from Ft. Kearny a faintly remembered dream, Edward felt thrilled to purchase dried fruit, a ham, and bacon to add to their dwindling food supply. Anything to relieve the monotony of boiled beans, three meals a day.

"The prices are outrageous!" declared another man. "Imagine flour for sale for ten dollars a sack, and bread twenty-nine cents a pound!"

"Well," reasoned Edward, "consider the time and expense of transporting goods from the Missouri River all the way out here."

The man muttered and mumbled his displeasure, but then, with a grimace, nodded his head in agreement.

In addition to taking on supplies, the pioneers welcomed the time to wash clothes, cook ahead, and repack their wagons, which were, after all, hardly bigger inside than the space of a double bed and a wardrobe.

The blacksmith kept busy from sunup to dark, shoeing horses and mules. Richard, Lewis, Edward, and the others also went over their wagons, checking wheels, and every inch of the body, replacing any wood that had started to split or break.

Edward also took this opportunity to write another article for *The Argus.* The folks back in Greencastle would be hard put to realize the wagons had been traveling for nearly two months without seeing signs of permanent human habitation beyond the Indian Mission, Ft. Kearny, and now, Ft. Laramie.

Sunday, the day of rest, became a serious matter. Not just their animals, but the pioneers also, needed to fortify themselves for the journey ahead.

Edward and the others attended church inside the fort. An army chaplain gave the sermon and an enlisted man thumped out the hymns on a spinet piano.

O God, our help in ages past,
Our hope for years to come,

As they sang, Edward felt the familiar words take on a new meaning for him and the friends on either side.

Our shelter from the stormy blast,

And our eternal home.

* * *

The next day, Edward wrote: *Monday, June 24 Leave Fort Laramie, the last civilized place between here and the West Coast. God help us.*

Chapter Sixteen

All semblances of prairie disappeared as they left Fort Laramie and entered the Laramie Mountains. An easy road through a barren landscape soon gave way to a rough and rocky route, cut through by ravines.

As promised by Ware's book, seven miles from the fort, the road descended a long, steep hill.

"Everyone gather round," came the shout from Captain Weston Clark.

As the fifty or so men walked to the front, Edward thought it a shame there wasn't any grass for the animals to eat as they waited for the wagons to move.

"We'll let one wagon at a time go down. Besides the driver, one man should walk with each wagon's mules or oxen, to keep them steady. Check your brakes before you start. We can't let the weight of the wagons push the animals. If they fall, we could lose both."

When the first wagon finally reached the bottom without incident, the entire population of the train—having been holding its breath—took a deep sigh of relief and then let loose a cheer.

Four miles farther on down the rocky road, they came to a steep ascent listed in the book. They lightened the wagons, carrying what they could, abandoning what they must. Sharing animals to double-team up the road, men had to lend a shoulder to get some wagons over the rough patches.

"Watch the curve!" yelled Clark. "Here's the sudden turn Ware warned us about."

One by one, they maneuvered the frightening ascent—and the even more dangerous descent—that followed.

We're definitely, *not* on the prairie, Edward thought.

❋ ❋ ❋

Although they had left the Platte River at Fort Laramie, there were occasional springs and streams. The biggest concern, outside of the condition and steepness of the road, was the lack of grass for the animals. When they stopped for mid-day lunch, and again to camp at night, they often had to walk the stock as much as a mile from the road to find fodder.

Two days later, Wednesday, June twenty-sixth, by Edward's journal, they camped by the side of the thirty-foot wide La Bonte River. It was a fine camping place with, at last, grass as well as plenty of water for the animals.

"Enjoy it this evening," Edward warned. "The book says, *In the next thirteen miles the chances for camping are poor; the road is but tolerably good."*

And so it went, day after day. Helping each other over the rough and dangerous patches—enjoying the occasional respites when a camping place provided grass and water—the hardy men, women, and children progressed through the dry landscape. Colorful, flat-topped mountains, carved by wind and flash floods surrounded them. On and on they trudged, climbing ever westward.

❊ ❊ ❊

"Remind me why I left home and Elizabeth, to wear out my boots walking to California," demanded Lewis as he and Edward walked next to their wagon. Richard drove the oxen.

"It seems to me," Edward replied, "you'd been talking about finding enough gold to buy your own farm. Or have you changed your mind about not wanting to move in with your folks? About having to live with your bride in the same bedroom you had when you were a kid?"

"No. I do *not* want to live with my folks. Work like a hired hand on their farm.

"But, I miss Elizabeth so much. I read the letter she gave me when we left, every night. I stroke the lock of hair she put in the envelope and long to run my fingers through the rest of that hair. I ache to hold her in my arms. Hear her voice. I'm not sure I can survive for two or three years without her."

"Would you want her to go through what Nancy did? Give birth on the trail? And walk, carrying her baby, all the way to California?"

Lewis shook his head. "Never!"

He looked at Edward. "What about you? Are you missing your Susanna as much as I am Elizabeth?'

Edward's thoughts immediately returned to the day when he had told Susanna he was going to California…

❊❊❊

Telling Susanna, it turned out, was even harder than telling his parents. The very next afternoon, he'd called on the Collins' and asked permission to take a walk with their daughter.

He and Susanna sauntered down Columbia Street toward Big Walnut River. He placed a hand under her elbow as their feet stirred up the dust. Passing the blacksmith's, Edward raised his hat in greeting.

They stopped in the shade of a tree and watched the river flow by. Here the air was only slightly cooler.

"Susanna, I need to tell you," Edward swallowed, "I'm going to California. It's certain. We'll leave next spring."

At Susanna's continued silence, he mumbled, "I just wanted you to know."

"I… I thought maybe you were… were…" She swallowed, tears welling in her eyes. "…going to propose marriage."

Caught completely off guard, Edward couldn't think of a thing to say.

"I was so sure." The tears spilled down her cheeks. "I even knew who I was going to ask to be my bridesmaids…"

Edward reached out to her.

"Don't." She pushed his hand aside. Shook her head. Turned away.

Edward felt like the most despicable kind of heel. In his excitement, he'd never stopped to consider what Susanna might expect.

"I never truly thought you'd go." She pulled her gaze from the river to look him in the eyes. "I never thought *anyone* I knew would go so far away."

He resisted the impulse to wipe the tears from her cheeks.

Thoughts flitted through Edward's head. *Wait for me. I'll be back. But what if I don't come back? I love you. But do I? What if I return to find I don't want to marry you? What could I tell you that I might not regret, even more, some day?*

"Susanna, I know California is a long way away, and that I can't *promise* to come back to Greencastle. I want you to always be my friend, even as I will always be yours. But, I can't ask you to wait for me. I can't promise to return and marry you. And, I won't promise something I can't be sure of fulfilling."

"Don't. Don't say anything. I know you don't love me the way I love you. You'd rather go to California than marry me."

"Please, Susanna! Don't cry." He was about to say, 'I love you,' but choked on the words. "All I can say for now is that you are very special to me."

"That's not enough," Susanna cried. "Not nearly enough."

⁂ ⁂ ⁂

Edward turned to Lewis. "After the way I bungled our leave-taking, Susanna may not even speak to me when we get home, let alone marry me."

Lewis looked surprised.

"I really messed up!" Edward admitted.

Chapter Seventeen

After endless miles of alkaline springs and lakes, with thin grass and no fuel other than wild sage, they arrived at the swiftly-moving Sweet Water River. Lush grass grew on the banks. What a relief to have fresh water for both people and animals!

"I know it's only Wednesday," Caroline said, but I do wish we could stay here tomorrow."

"Let's ask Captain Clark," Richard said.

"Well," Clark said in reply, "We occasionally have to keep moving on a Sunday, because there's no fodder for the animals, or the water's bad. So why *can't* we have a Sabbath rest on Wednesday? After all, God made all of the days; it's only man who organized them into a calendar."

"Besides," Edward added, "I'd like some time to explore Independence Rock."

And so, the others in the wagon train agreeing, they made camp that evening for a two-night stay.

Early the next morning, most of the pioneers hiked to Independence Rock. Named years before by explorers who had camped there on the Fourth of July, the immense rock dominated the skyline from several miles away.

"From the distance, it looked like a steamboat," commented Caroline to no one in particular. "But now it just looks *huge.*"

"Look!" cried Richard, "people have carved their names and dates on it."

Edward felt a thrill of excitement run through his body. "Do you realize what date *this* is?" he asked.

A general murmuring greeted his question.

"I think it's July something..."

"You mean it's not still June?"

"I know it's not Sunday!"

When the comments dwindled into silence, Edward announced, "Today is the Fourth of July!"

"The Fourth of July?"

"Independence Day!"

"Hip, hip, hurray!"

"We *must* celebrate."

"We the People of the United States—" began a voice.

"—in Order to form a more perfect Union..." the others joined in, reciting the well-remembered words to the Preamble to the Constitution.

"Here we are," Edward said to Caroline, "deep in the Indian Territories, far from the United States, commemorating the Fourth of July."

"This isn't anything like Fourth of July at home," she replied, "with picnics and patriotic speeches. Flags and bunting decorating the band stand... but Lord, it *does* feel good!"

"It feels right," Edward agreed.

"—do ordain and establish this Constitution for the United States of America."

Breaking the silence that followed, a woman's voice led out strongly:

Oh, say can you see,

by the dawn's early light,

The rest joined in, standing tall, hands over hearts.

What so proudly we hailed

at the twilight's last gleaming?

The hot sun beat down on bonnets and slouch hats as voices rang out, singing with fervor many had not experienced for a long, long time.

O'er the land of the free and the home of the brave.

After a moment of respectful silence, the mood changed as a man sang out,

Yankee Doodle went to town

Riding on a pony...

With a shout of approval, everyone joined in. Soon, three boys about eight years old started marching back and forth between the pioneers and the monolithic rock, waving their caps in the air.

Mind the music and the step,

And with the girls be handy.

Ten-year-old Ellen, hand in hand with Hannah Clark, joined the parade, along with several other boys. Everyone began clapping as they sang.

And there they had a swampin' gun,

As big as a log of maple,

Upon a deuced little cart,

A load for father's cattle.

Little Lucy Kelsey ran up to Ellen and Hannah. They each grabbed one of her hands, and the three of them were part of the parade. Verse after verse rang in the crystal air.

And every time they fired it off

It took a horn of powder;

It made a noise like father's gun,

Only a nation louder.

"Hurrah!" everyone shouted as the song finally came to an end. Hats sailed high into the cobalt sky. Women hugged each other. For just a few minutes, they were no longer forty wagons crossing an uninhabited, frequently forbidding, wasteland, but a community. A small town, celebrating the 4th of July.

"We must add our names to the rock!" someone suggested.

"Yes, yes!" others responded.

"And the date!" Edward shouted, feeling himself being carried along with the tide of patriotic emotion. "This is an historic occasion. An epic event!"

"Yes, the date," the others agreed.

"Years and years from now," intoned Richard, "people will visit this rock and see our names carved on its face. And they will know we celebrated Independence Day, 1850, right here."

"It *is* an historic occasion," repeated one of the men. "And we are all a part of it!"

❊❊❊

As they walked back to their campsite, Ellen took Edward's hand and said, "I almost wish we could stay here forever. This was the most fun day we've had on the whole trip."

There was a murmuring of agreement.

"Today *was* nice," Edward said. "Especially since tomorrow's destination is named Devil's Gate. Now *that* sounds ominous!"

Chapter Eighteen

The next day they arrived at Devil's Gate in the Rattlesnake Hills. The 'Gate' was a singular fissure in vertical granite, with walls towering some four hundred feet into the air. The Sweet Water River, roiling and foaming, forced its way through at the foot of the chasm.

"My, will you look at that," Mary Ann marveled, her heart thumping. "It's the grandest thing I've ever seen."

"It looks," Caroline continued, "like God reached down from the farthest corners of the universe, and with one stroke of His hand, cleaved the whole huge piece in two."

"And the river," added Nancy, "rushed into the gorge, singing praises to the Lord God and His creation."

❊ ❊ ❊

A few moments later, Edward looked over and saw all three ladies, plus young Ellen and little Lucy, their shoes and stockings on the nearby riverbank, bathing their feet in the cool, tumbling water of the Sweet Water River.

Just seeing their enjoyment made *his* feet, tightly laced in their heavy boots, feel unbearably hot. These feet had walked the better part of nearly eight hundred miles. They cried out to be released, to soak in the river.

He looked around. A few other females up and down the riverbank also had their bare feet in the water. But, there wasn't a man among them.

With a sigh, he turned his back on the inviting scene, and finished setting up their camp and getting supper started.

❋ ❋ ❋

Saturday, July 13, 1850, Edward wrote in his journal. *Arrive at South Pass.*

They stopped their wagons on a plain, with two hills of the same elevation on each side.

"According to Ware's book," Edward said, "those two low hills mark South Pass." He squinted as he peered into the distance. From here it's sort of hard to see the Continental Divide, where all the rivers on the west flow into the Pacific, and on the east, into the Mississippi."

"The climb has been so gradual," said William, who had walked up to join Edward's wagon, "I didn't even realize we'd reached the summit." He stood, an arm around Nancy, and holding Lucy by the hand.

Caroline and Ellen joined them.

Edward said, "Ellen, why don't you get Hannah, and see if you can find a place between two streams, one flowing west and one flowing east. That will be the Continental Divide."

Ellen and Hannah, with Lucy trotting along beside them, scurried in circles. "Here it is!" Ellen cried out. "That stream is going one direction," she pointed, "and the one over there, is flowing the other way."

"Do you know what that means?" asked William.

Ellen shook her head.

By now Hannah and Lucy had joined them. "What does it mean?" Hannah asked.

"From this minute on, every creek, every stream, every river we pass, will be flowing into the Pacific Ocean!"

"Tomorrow's the Sabbath," said Caroline. "We'll celebrate God's creation on the top of the Continental Divide."

Chapter Nineteen

Two days later they arrived at a fork in the road.

"Circle up!" Wagon Captain, Weston Clark called out.

When everyone had gathered around, Clark announced, "This is a major decision point in our journey." He pointed to the left where a clearly discernable dirt road led off to the southwest.

"This fork is a good road to Fort Bridger and then on to Salt Lake City. Or, at Fort Bridger you can choose to turn north to Soda Springs, and then Fort Hall, also on a pretty good road. After Fort Hall there's a choice to go southwest to California and gold, or northwest to Oregon with free land to homestead and farm."

"What's on the right fork?" asked Richard.

"The right fork takes five days off the travel time to California by way of Sublette's Cut Off," Clark answered. "Unfortunately, it also promises a poor excuse for a road, and at least thirty-five miles—without one drop of water.

"Those who wish to continue on down from Fort Bridger to Salt Lake City," Clark added, have the additional enticement of a city with homes and farms, fresh fruits and vegetables." He paused, "And Mormons."

"I don't want nothin' to do with Mormons," commented a man standing toward the back of the group.

"They might not be so bad," another responded, "even if they do practice polygamy."

"Fresh fruits and vegetables sound really good along about now," came a woman's voice, answered by murmurs of affirmation.

"We'll camp here for tonight," Clark concluded. "You can discuss your choices. We'll meet in the morning to split up, if that's what you decide to do."

***

That night, William and Nancy Kelsey with little Lucy, along with Frank and Mary Ann Ashley, still carrying baby Joshua in his papoose, walked over to where Edward, Richard, and Lewis were sharing a campfire with Caroline Gould and Ellen.

"Frank and me, we need to talk to you," announced William rather abruptly.

The tone of his voice sent Edward's feelings scattering like prairie dogs diving for their holes. "What have you decided?" he asked.

"Well, you see," said Frank, his arm around his wife, "it's like this. Me an' Mary Ann have decided to change course. Take the Fort Bridger Road to Salt Lake City. We'll rest up there. Repair the wagon. The brakes are near worn out. And we both need new boots.

"An' then," he continued, "we've decided to go to *Oregon,* instead of California!"

"But... but, whatever for?" sputtered Lewis. Edward felt the same shock.

"The hardest part of the journey to California is still ahead," Frank said. "Sublette's Cut Off—miles without water. Or an even longer trip, and no matter what, even more places without water before you get to the Sierra Nevada Mountains. And *they* make South Pass and the Rockies seem like child's play. That's no trip to take with a newborn baby."

"And besides," added Mary Ann, "Oregon has good farmland for the asking. It would be a nice place to bring up a family."

"Anyways, with so many others headin' for California," continued Frank, "there's likely no gold left in them hills."

"But, you were *planning* on going to California," said Lewis.

"And there'll be gold left," urged Edward. "There's *gotta* be!"

"You can't leave us *now!"* cried Ellen.

Frank looked at William who was clearing his throat. "Nancy and I have decided to go with them to Salt Lake and then on to Oregon," stated William. "It does sound like a better place than the Mother Lode for a young family."

He looked at Nancy, who smiled and nodded.

"You see," he continued. "We're going to have another baby."

"Oh, Nancy!" Caroline jumped up and went over to hug her. "I am so pleased for you. While no one can take Caleb's place, another baby is wonderful. Just what you've needed."

"Anyway," William continued, "we figured we'd best tell you tonight. In case either of you decided to come along."

Frank added, "We're going to claim land next to each other. Sort of join families."

"And, we'd love to have you come, too," finished William. "Make it a real family—with all of you."

Edward had been watching and listening, feeling dismayed. He'd enjoyed the camaraderie of the four wagons over all those miles, but he had his heart set on going all the way to California. To see the Mother Lode. To find gold. To experience, and write first-hand about this monumental event in history.

Suddenly he had a horrible thought. *What if Richard and Lewis decide to go to Oregon? Richard was more interested in the trip than its outcome. And Lewis wants a farm of his own. He might choose to go to Oregon and send for Elizabeth to join him there.*

"What do you think, E. B.? Lewis?" Richard asked, one eyebrow cocked.

Edward looked at Lewis. *What will he decide?*

Lewis answered without even having to think about it. "I started for gold in California. I aim to finish doing just that."

"My thoughts, exactly!" Edward felt almost light-headed with relief.

"Well, I guess that's it for this wagon," Richard declared. "What about you ladies?" He looked at Caroline.

She took Ellen into her arms. The child looked ready to burst into tears. "Well?" she asked.

"I don't know," Ellen wailed.

"Well then, I do!" Caroline sounded firm. "We'll just keep going. See what all the fuss is about—in California."

"Thanks for asking," said Richard, "but it looks like these two wagons are going to California."

"If you decide to take the Fort Bridger road," William continued, "we could stay together another couple of days."

"It's a *much* easier road," Frank added.

"But," Richard responded, "it also adds five more days to the trip. Nearly a week!"

"Why don't you think about it?" asked William. "You can tell us what you decide in the morning."

As Edward was following his cousin and friend to their own wagon, Ellen walked over, looking devastated.

He knelt, looking her eye to eye. "What's the matter, little one?"

Tears began to run down her cheeks. "You, you said... you said we'd all be fa-family." She was crying in earnest now. "Th-that I'd never be left alone!"

"Well now, I did say that."

"And first Mister Wilson and George left. And those two brothers."

"And now," agreed Edward, "Kelseys and Ashleys have decided to go to Oregon."

"Who's left to take care of *me?*"

"Your mother seems to be doing a really good job of that."

"But... but what if?"

"You've still got my cousin Richard, and my friend Lewis, and—"

"But *they* don't take any notice of me. Only you do."

"So, okay. You've still got me."

At Ellen's sad shake of a head, he added, "And I have no intention or going off on my own..." he tried to smile reassuringly, "or let anything bad happen to you, or me."

Chapter Twenty

"We've still got to decide whether to take Sublette's Cut Off or not," said Richard as they were preparing to bed down.

"I say we take the Cut Off," Lewis said. "We've already poked along more than necessary."

"But," objected Edward, remembering Ellen's tears, "what if Caroline wants to take the Fort Bridger road?"

"Well, let her," said Lewis.

"We're not glued to Widow Gould and her child," agreed Richard.

"Yes we are," argued Edward. "We can't just leave them on their own, after all this time."

"That widow and her child would still be with other wagons, not on their own," Lewis responded.

"But, I promised Ellen."

"*What* did you promise?" asked Richard.

"That we'd not leave her.

"Why'd you do that?" asked Lewis.

"When her father died, she was terrified no one would take care of her if anything happened to her mother."

"And I suppose you offered to adopt her," said Richard. "Take her on for the rest of your life!"

"Well, no. Not exactly."

"Well then," Lewis chimed in, "what, *exactly* did you mean?"

"I don't know... Anyway, I'll talk to her mother in the morning. Maybe they're planning to take Sublette's Cut Off, and there won't *be* any problem."

* * *

Clark called the meeting early the next morning. "There are decisions for each of you to make," he shouted. "I would certainly advise against taking Sublette's Cut Off if you are using horses. They just don't have the stamina.

"Some of you will elect to take the main road to Fort Bridger and then back up to Fort Hall. Those of you, and any others who decide to go on to Salt Lake City, can leave whenever you wish. The road is easy and clearly marked."

Edward looked around. It seemed several people were going to take the road. He searched for Caroline and Ellen, but couldn't see them in the crush.

"But if you decide to take the Cut Off," the captain continued, "rest this morning. Be sure your animals get plenty of grass and water. Eat a hearty dinner at noon.

"Plan to line up and leave around four o'clock this afternoon, when the worst heat of the day begins to ease off. Then, walk all night, and you should arrive at water and a place to camp by mid-morning tomorrow. Don't stop along the way."

"What if a wagon breaks down?" came a shout from the group.

"The others won't be able to stop and help you."

"Isn't that a little cruel?"

"Yes, it is. But if any of the animals stop walking, they might not be *able* to start again. And anyone who doesn't reach water by midmorning—will *die.* Any other questions?"

Silence.

"What are *you* going to do?" asked one of the men.

"We're taking the Fort Bridger-Fort Hall road to California," Clark said. "I've got a wife and young daughter to think about. Any of you who want to, are welcome to come along."

The farewells occasioned handshakes, hugs, and tears. Edward knew, as he shook William's hand, they'd most likely never see any of them again. Wouldn't even have an address to exchange letters.

Edward joined Caroline and Ellen as the crowd began to disperse. After the captain's talk, he didn't hold out much hope they'd want to take the Cut Off.

"I think we'd be wiser to go to Fort Bridger," Caroline said as if in answer to his thoughts. "What about you?"

"Richard and Lewis are determined to take the cutoff," Edward admitted.

"Are... are you going with them?" asked Ellen.

"Ellen! For goodness sake! This is a decision for adults to make. I'm ashamed of you," Caroline scolded.

A thousand arguments ran through Edward's head.

Richard is family. Lewis my best friend. We started out together, pooling resources. If we don't stay together now, how can we possibly meet up when we get to California?

"I made you a promise, and I'll keep it, even if it means leaving Richard and Lewis, and moving my stuff into your wagon."

Where did those words come from?

Ellen's smile just about broke his heart. But he dreaded what Richard and Lewis would say when they heard.

"If it was just up to me," Caroline said, "I wouldn't think twice about taking Sublette's Cut Off, but I have to think about my daughter. I'm responsible for her wellbeing."

"I understand," Edward said. "I'm sure Richard and Lewis will be upset, but I just can't let the two of you go off on your own."

"Much as I feel bound to you by bonds of friendship, we won't be entirely alone if we take the Fort Bridger Road. We'll be with the Clarks—and Hannah."

Edward suddenly realized *he* didn't want to go on without Caroline and Ellen. Where did *that* thought come from?

Ellen was looking at the ground. All Edward could see of her were the top of her bonnet, and the circling of one small, scuffed boot stirring up the dust.

Finally she looked up. "Why *can't* we go with Mister Daingerfield on Sublette's Cut Off?"

Caroline smiled and shook her head. "Wouldn't you like to be with Hannah?"

"Yes. But I'd rather be with Mister Daingerfield."

"Do you really think you could stay awake? Walk for eighteen or twenty hours without stopping?"

"I'm a big girl. You keep telling me so. I can do it."

Her mother shrugged her shoulders in mock despair. "You heard the lady. I guess we're taking the Cut Off."

Chapter Twenty-One

"Momma, I'm thirsty."

Edward, from the bench of Caroline's wagon, heard the softly spoken words clearly. He had offered to drive the oxen while Caroline and Ellen walked beside the wagon. Of the seventy wagons that had left Fort Kearny almost exactly two months ago, only twelve had chosen to take Sublette's Cut Off. And Ellen was the only child.

The small train had been moving across the barren wasteland for about five hours. The sun had just slipped below the horizon, and the evening sky was a pearlescent coral, tinged with deepening blue.

Edward felt sorry for Caroline. He knew, instinctively, what was going through her mind.

Why did I let Ellen sway my decision? She'll never make it through the whole night and into tomorrow.

Edward heard her say, "Try this." He glanced over and saw her hand Ellen a small, washed pebble. "Suck on it to keep your mouth wet."

"Thank you."

"You're welcome."

On and on, through the endless night, Edward drove the oxen, wincing with each jounce of the steel-rimmed wheels into a rut or over a rock. His head ached. His back ached. His posterior felt bruised and battered. And he, too, was thirsty.

❋ ❋ ❋

"Momma, it doesn't work anymore."

Twilight had deepened into night some time ago. It happened gradually, but they could still see where they were going as the white moon rose majestically in the starry sky.

"What doesn't work anymore?"

"The pebble. My mouth is so dry."

Edward could hear Caroline's thoughts as clearly as he heard Ellen's voice.

Mister Gould, why did you have to die? I know you couldn't help it. You were just helping another child, just the way you helped my Ellen—and me. And Ellen is, has always been, my responsibility, not yours. But, why did you die? I don't think I can I do this alone.

"Put the stone in your pocket so you don't swallow it," she said, "and take a sip of water." Continuing to walk as the oxen pulled ever onward, Edward heard Caroline lift the lid of their water bucket, bound to the side of the wagon, and dip in a cup.

"Take one mouthful, but don't swallow right away. Just hold it. Let your mouth feel the moisture. Then you can let it go down your throat."

"Oh, momma, that was *delicious!*"

"Do that one more time, and I'll sip what's left. Then suck on the pebble for another while now."

❋ ❋ ❋

Some time after midnight—the moon was beginning its descent—Edward heard shouting coming from someone several wagons ahead.

"Get up, you galldarned horse! Get the hell up!"

Edward shivered in the cold as he heard the sound of a whip slashing the poor animal's hide.

Wagons ahead of his were detouring around the problem.

"Get up, I say! Damned lazy animal!"

By the time the wagon Edward was driving reached the problem, the man had taken the yoke off the animal lying on the ground. The poor beast huffed and wheezed, trying helplessly to get up.

"Damned horse. Get outa my way. I'll pull the galldarned wagon myself!"

Edward watched in amazement as the man put the yoke on his own shoulders. He poked the skinny, shivering horse still standing next to him with his whip handle, and strained to get the wagon rolling again.

"Pull, you lazy beast! I can't do it all by myself."

Edward thought the man might have a stroke, pulling with all his might. But the heavy wagon wheels didn't move.

"Nellie! Get off the wagon and push!"

A tiny woman clambered off the wagon seat and put her shoulder to the back of the wagon.

No motion.

Edward felt his heart lurch in sympathy. Not for the man, who had been warned not to try the Cut Off with horses, but for the doomed animals themselves. And the man's wife.

What will happen to them? If the horses are lucky, they'll be shot. Put out of their misery. The crazy bastard can't just leave them there to die, slowly, from dehydration, can he?

And what of his wife?

"Give it up, old man," Edward heard from the wagon behind him. "Take your wife and whatever water you can carry and start walking."

"I'll be damned if I'll leave my wagon!"

"Well, give your wife some water and let *her* join us."

A few minutes later Edward heard two distinct gunshots. And then one more.

But, he thought, *there were only two horses.*

Edward knew there was no way to find out what had happened until they made camp.

If they made it to camp.

Chapter Twenty-Two

The animals picked up the scent of water at midmorning. Since daybreak their pace had gradually slowed. They'd plodded, heads down, tongues flopping. But now, they moved faster without any urging from Edward or the other drivers.

When they reached the Green River, two hundred and fifty feet wide, Edward un-yoked the oxen and let them loose to drink the life-giving water. Soon, all the animals were clustered together, downriver from the wagons, while the people gathered upstream. Some people dipped cups and ladles into the cold, crystal clear water, while others knelt on the banks, used their hands as scoops, and slurped up the heaven-sent liquid.

Finally, thirst satisfied, Edward and the others staked the animals to graze in what grasses there were along the river.

"I don't know whether I'm more hungry or sleepy," he commented. "But I *do* know, I don't want to sit on a hard wagon bench again any time soon!"

Sleep won out. Soon, men, women, and children were bedded down in the shade of their wagons, passed out from exhaustion.

Edward awoke as the sun was slipping into afternoon. He felt groggy from sleeping through the heat of the day, but still not rested. Hunger was a thundering demand.

Stumbling, he started a fire to heat water for coffee. Rummaged in the back of the wagon for a kettle of cold beans. Found a package of stone-hard biscuits.

Around him, others were doing likewise.

A woman's figure drifted past him, catching the corner of his eye. He looked up. She was thin, her faded and worn dress hung limply on her frame. The equally faded sunbonnet hid her face. Then she turned. Her eyes stared through him as if he weren't there.

Nellie! The tiny wife from the doomed wagon of last night.

She looked around, a lost soul, and then glided onward, as though her feet weren't even touching the ground.

Edward watched her pass. First Caroline, and then two other ladies went out to her. Touched her shoulder. Guided her to a place in the shade to sit down. Handed her a cup of water. Murmured to her in low voices.

Edward looked around, but could see nothing of her wagon or her crazy husband. *The third shot! At least he had the good sense to shoot himself, rather than his wife. I wonder what will happen to her now, poor thing.*

For the rest of the journey, Nellie followed the wagon train like some mongrel dog that had been kicked by its master. The men kept an eye on her, to keep her out of danger if they could. The women handed her plates of food, cups of water. She ate and drank what was given.

She slept wherever she was offered a blanket to roll up in. When the women went to the river to bathe, she joined them, returning in a dry dress and apron someone had loaned her.

Nellie never had talked much. Hadn't laughed. Hadn't sung and gossiped with the others. Now, she was completely mute.

Although he knew he'd never learn her ultimate outcome, Edward would never forget the poor unfortunate creature. She'd become just one of several people he'd met on the trail whose stories he couldn't write up for the *Argus*. They'd met, shared a portion of the adventure, and then parted, with no sense of resolution to their tale.

❊ ❊ ❊

In the days to come, the wagon train followed rivers, where there were any. They made more night crossings, some of them longer journeys without water than Sublette's Cut Off. But none was as frightening. Now they knew what to expect. Knew what they could endure.

Chapter Twenty-Three

Sunday, August 4, 1850, Edward wrote in his journal. *Spent the day at a river called St. Mary's, by some, and by others, the Humboldt. We will follow the Humboldt River until we get to the last, really terrible desert.*

Over and over again, the valley of the Humboldt narrowed, and the road was forced to cross the river. At these places the river also became deep and swiftly moving.

Edward was driving his wagon at one of the crossings, when the oxen balked at going into the churning water. "Come on, Clyde. You can do it!" he called out, snapping the whip over the lead oxen's head.

"Hold on!" he admonished Ellen. She sat beside him on the ride across the river, gripping the wagon bench. Meanwhile, her mother followed behind them on *their* wagon, which Richard was driving.

Lewis remained on the bank, helping others prepare to cross.

Edward's wagon swayed as the river pushed up against it. For what seemed like forever, the wagon floated while the oxen swam frantically in the current. *Finally,* the oxen gained firmer footing, and the wagon wheels touched bottom again.

"Good boys!" he cheered as the oxen lumbered up the other bank. "I *knew* you could make it!"

He pulled the wagon up, out of the way. Leaving Ellen sitting on the bench, he went back to watch as Richard and Caroline made the dangerous crossing.

He'd just reached the edge of the river when he saw one of Caroline's oxen slip and fall. Richard pulled on the reins with all his strength. "Whoa!"

"Oh, my Lord, have mercy," Caroline prayed out loud.

Water rushed around the wagon and struggling animals. "Edward! Can you help?" Richard cried.

"I'll try!"

Edward gasped as cold water rose to his chest, threatening to pull him under and, at the same time, wash him down stream.

Laboriously, Edward made his way—half walking, half swimming—to the middle of the river. Lunging, he grabbed the lead oxen's yoke, as much to save himself as to urge the animal up on his feet.

Miraculously, he felt the beast gain a foothold. With Edward pulling and Richard urging them on they, at last, all managed to finish the crossing.

Edward leaned over with his hands on his knees, gasping for breath, while Richard drove the frightened animals farther up the bank.

"Thank you, Richard!" Edward heard Caroline say. "You were *wonderful.* I could just imagine our wagon tipping over. Being dashed to pieces. All our possessions lost. The oxen drowned. I don't know how to thank you enough."

"Don't thank me, Widow Gould. Thank my cousin. He did the dangerous part."

She jumped off the wagon bench and rushed to Edward. Without a pause, she threw her arms around him, completely overlooking the fact he was sopping wet.

"Thank *you,* dear Edward," she gushed.

Edward's arms involuntarily went around her. He was both stunned and surprised. He'd never seen Caroline hug anyone but Ellen. Not even her husband!

As he felt Caroline against his wet shirt and pants, he was shocked to feel his own body suddenly react as if someone like Susannah were hugging him. It certainly wasn't like being hugged by Aunt Jane!

"I'm sorry—" he started.

At the same moment, Caroline pulled back and began to stutter. "Go... goodness! Wh... whatever... possessed..."

Edward pulled his arms around himself, as he began to shiver, whether from cold or embarrassment he couldn't say.

Meanwhile Caroline clasped her hands to her breast, as if in prayer. "I can't thank you enough for saving my wagon. That was a very brave thing you did. Going into the water, and all."

Then, reverting to the motherly concern she normally displayed, she ordered, "Now, you just go back to your own wagon and get some dry clothing."

Neither of them would ever mention the incident again. But, that night Edward dreamt of Susannah.

✻ ✻ ✻

Finally the muddy Humboldt ended with a whimper, into a marsh of bulrushes and salt incrustations. They had arrived at Humboldt Sink.

"Good heavens!" Caroline exclaimed, "That is the *worst* thing I've *ever* smelled!"

"Even worse than rotten eggs," agreed Edward.

Ellen just held her nose and grimaced.

"Not only is the *marsh* disgusting," Richard commented, "—obviously unusable by man or beast—but worse still, the *next* forty miles have to be covered in one stretch. There's no grass or usable water for the whole distance."

Chapter Twenty-Four

The trek from Humboldt Sink to the foot of the Sierras was a nightmare out of hell. Edward's impressions were of people and animals plodding, one foot in front of the other. Without will. Barely conscious.

They walked, because to do otherwise meant death.

On the second day, when the pioneers stopped for their midday dinner, and to rest through the hottest part of the day, one of the oxen dropped to its knees. It belonged to two brothers from Wisconsin, Sven and Peter Ohlson.

"I been takin' off da yoke," Sven said with his Norwegian accent, "an' into the dust, he yust dropped." Sven shook his head, looking sad.

"Da oxen," added Peter, a gentle blond giant, like his brother, "more dead dey look, den alive."

Edward had to agree. 'Gaunt' didn't begin to describe their condition.

Richard arrived at the Ohlson's wagon. "You should put those poor beasts out of their misery," he advised.

"Ya," Sven said, "I t'ink so too."

"Den, what we do wit..." Peter's gesture encompassed their wagon, indicating all their worldly goods.

Edward put a comforting hand on Peter's shoulder. "Sort through your things. Put all your food and water on the ten wagons that are left. Bundle what clothing you can carry on your backs. We'll see what of your tools we can distribute among the rest of us..."

By the time the oxen were mercifully killed, and the Ohlson's possessions packed, distributed, or abandoned, the pioneers had little appetite for a cold dinner.

"I have an idea," Edward said. "I put a pot of beans to soak day before yesterday, planning on cooking them for dinner. But we haven't seen so much as a twig for a fire. Why don't we chop up the Ohlson's wagon and burn the wood for cooking?"

"We have a pot of beans soaking, too," said one wife.

"Same here," said someone else.

"We can *all* cook a hot meal over the same fire," Richard said.

❋ ❋ ❋

During the next couple of days, the small wagon train passed shallow graves, more debris of abandoned possessions, and decaying remains of whole dead animals.

The stench of rotting flesh made Edward gag. He tasted the bitter eruption of vomit rising in his throat. Immediately pinching his nose closed and swallowing rapidly, he just barely managed to contain it.

Others were doing the same, while some couldn't help themselves, and added another layer to the disgusting odor.

By night and day, they were surrounded by the specter of death. Even the ribs of the abandoned coverless wagons seemed skeletal. Not a leaf or a stem graced the hard gray landscape. The bleached and whitened bones of long-dead animals glistened horribly in the fitful starlight, as they traveled at night.

At last, what was left of the wagon train limped into Ragtown, the first city they had seen since leaving St. Joseph. In later years, Edward would smile at that inauspicious name for what would become Carson City.

Their provisions were nearly gone. The wagons that had made it this far were falling apart. People and animals were little better.

Edward had to ask a man in town what day it was, to write in his journal.

Wednesday, August 14, arrived in Rag Town. Rested today. Bought fresh vegetables, the first we've had since leaving St. Joseph three and a half months ago. Need to repair our wagons. The sight of the High Sierra peaks, still snow covered against the deep blue sky, fills me with both wonder and dread.

Chapter Twenty-Five

"I would love to spend about a month here," Edward said, "just sleeping and eating!"

Caroline looked with fond nostalgia at the town. "I think I could spend a lifetime here just to see houses with porches and vegetable gardens again. Corn on the cob, peas, beans, onions." She stood there, eyes closed, a blissful look on her face.

"You aren't serious!"

She sighed. "I am so tired of barren desert. This valley, with the Carson River tumbling through it, nourishes my soul."

"And," commented Richard, "I'll bet you everything we have, the High Sierras look better over there—waaay over there—than they will close up and climbing."

Caroline shuddered. "I don't know if I've got it in me to make that one last push."

"Don't talk like that!" Edward admonished. "We all feel that way now, but we're so close. We can do it. We've *got* to!"

* * *

The next day they began emptying each of the ten wagons, sorting and stacking belongings in their camping area next to the Carson River. The women and a couple of younger boys took turns watching the oxen luxuriously feeding on the tender grasses that grew there.

"Let me help you and Ellen empty out everything," Edward offered, "and I'll take your wagon in for repair."

"Yours still looks pretty good," Caroline said, "but I know we'll need new axels, and some of the wheel spokes replaced, at the very least."

"Richard and Lewis are taking care of ours. It needs some fixing up, too."

Even with the men and older boys helping, it took several days for the ten remaining beat up wagons to be made serviceable enough to contemplate crossing the Sierras.

A repair master supervised the repairs in his large, well-stocked, open-sided shed. The area was a beehive of activity, as blacksmith and wheelwright pounded, and men grunted and shouted to each other.

Edward and Richard met Ragtown's postmaster, Wes Mitchell. "If you'd like, when your train is up and running, 'Snowshoe' John Thompson can guide you over the Sierras," he said. "I can send him over to your camp, if you're interested."

"That sounds great," Richard said, "but isn't that an awfully big imposition?"

"Naw," Wes replied. "I have a sack of mail needing to be taken to Hangtown, anyway. Your train will slow him down some, but that don't make no never mind."

"How often does he make the trip?" Edward asked.

"Once a month during the summer. Takes mail for California and leaves it in Hangtown. Picks up eastbound mail there and brings it back. An army wagon from Fort Hall or Fort Bridger comes by for it about once a month.

"It's a bit more catch as catch can, come winter. But Thompson can still make it with snowshoes."

"I know I should send an article for our town newspaper," Edward said, shaking his head, "but I simply can't put pen to paper to describe Sublette's Cut-Off and the Humboldt Sink."

"Give it some time," Wes advised. "Once you're safe and sound in California, I bet you'll write a hum dinger of an article."

Edward smiled and shrugged his shoulders. "Maybe."

⁕ ⁕ ⁕

"Tomorrow, we begin climbing the Sierra Nevada Mountains," 'Snowshoe' announced to the pioneers two nights later.

"We already know that," Edward whispered to Richard. But still, hearing it put into words, made his heart drop.

Chapter Twenty-Six

The canyon leading up to the mountains was five miles of rocks and boulders. One by one, the wagons rolled over or threaded their way around and between stones. Some of the boulders were so high, the wagons tipped precariously. Men frantically held onto the other side to keep them from toppling over.

"When we bought the oxen and wagon, back in St. Joseph," Edward said to Richard with wonder, "who could have imagined what they would have to travel through?"

"And we aren't even there yet," his cousin replied. "But here we go!"

They had arrived at the first steep ascent. The train stopped and everyone stared.

"I guess we're about to crawl up the elephant's tail..." one of the men commented in awe.

"We'll double hitch all the oxen to the first five wagons," 'Snowshoe' directed. "When they all reach the top, we'll bring the animals back down for the last five.

"I'll ask two or three of you to help herd the oxen down, while the rest of you up there can prepare dinner for everyone, once we all get up."

"Will people from the last five wagons pay us for the food they eat?"

"Some people have to argue and complain about everything," Lewis muttered.

Edward nodded in complete agreement. He watched to see how 'Snowshoe' reacted to the challenge.

Even though they had offered to pay him a modest amount for going with them, Thompson could have been to Hangtown and back way more easily, and in less than half the time, than he would shepherding them all the way.

A slight frown and the tightening of his lips were all that showed his displeasure. In a calm voice he said, "After dinner, we'll go down a short, but very steep grade to a valley where we'll spend the night.

"Tomorrow, we'll switch the order for another steep ascent, and the those people can prepare dinner for you folks."

The others looked as relieved as Edward felt at the neat solution to what could have been a nagging problem.

"I can hardly believe the oxen will be able to haul the wagons up this steep a trail," panted Caroline, using a walking stick to pull herself up the narrow track. Everyone but the driver of each wagon had to climb the mountain. They carried whatever they could, tied in packs across their backs, to lighten the load on the wagons.

"I've never been prouder of our team than I am this morning," agreed Edward, walking beside her.

"And I can't believe you volunteered to make this climb twice in one day," she asserted.

"Well, I couldn't let Richard and Lewis outdo me."

"But Richard is driving *your* wagon, and Lewis is driving mine. You're walking."

"Oh well," Edward smiled and shrugged, " that's just the way it goes, I guess." He was having a hard time catching his breath. Maybe down and back up again in one day, wasn't such a good idea.

Caroline grinned. "The three of you volunteer for everything. And then there are others, who never offer."

When all ten wagons finally reached the top of the first steep incline, dinner was ready and waiting. It was a subdued affair, but at least there was enough food and water for both man and beast.

They all knew, this was but the first of several ascents they'd have to make in climbing the Sierras.

"Going down is going to be even more dangerous," Lewis muttered.

And it was.

One yoke of oxen was hitched to the wagon and as many men as could, caught hold of heavy chains attached to the back. When the wheels started rolling, they pulled to keep it from running down the mountain, killing the oxen, or tumbling over a cliff to be dashed into kindling wood.

Edward rode the brakes as hard as he could when he began the stomach-wrenching descent. "Easy boys," he comforted the oxen. "Take it slow and easy."

At the beginning, everything seemed under control. Then came yelling, as first one and then another of the men pulling on the chains, lost his footing in the dirt of the trail.

Edward cried out, his heart in his throat, as the wagon surged forward sickeningly, whacking into the ox team's haunches.

"Dig in! Dig in!" the men screamed. Finally their boots found purchase and the wagon's downward plunge slowed.

Sweat ran down Edwards face, stinging his eyes and dripping off his chin. He didn't dare let loose of the reins to wipe it off. "Good boys," he called out to the oxen.

"That had to hurt," he muttered. "But you didn't even flinch when you got hit." His heart swelled in gratitude.

"You are the best team of oxen in the world!" he exclaimed. "When we get to the camp for tonight, you deserve extra good food and a rub-down.

"But don't get too comfortable," he added, under his breath. "We've got to do the same thing—or worse—tomorrow.

"And the day after that."

Chapter Twenty-Seven

"Well E.B., we're sure not in Indiana anymore," Richard commented, as he and Edward trudged alongside the wagon Lewis was driving.

After several days of near-disastrous ascents and descents, the California foothills scenery mesmerized them. Tall grasses, bleached golden by the sun, waved in a gentle breeze. Large outcroppings of rocks looked as though a landscape artist had put them there. Groups of live oaks provided a touch of green and the promise of shade from the heat, while here and there tall pines stood as sentinels watching over all.

At the first sight of Hangtown, Edward could hardly believe they'd made it. The entire wagon train stopped. They stood, dazed expressions on their faces, mirroring what he knew was on his own.

They were a sorry-looking bunch. Wagons patched together with cannibalized bits and pieces from others that had fallen by the wayside. Surviving animals from broken-down wagons were pressed into service, pulling in the place of those that died—and been gratefully eaten—along the way. The people who shared the cobbled-together wagons and teams, were reduced to worn out clothes and patched boots. The remaining wagons had room for only the most essential goods and equipment.

By way of contrast, Hangtown fairly exploded with energy and barely suppressed excitement. The town—a chaotic mix of tents and shanties—seemed to barely cling to the hillsides. Several larger wooden buildings crowded along a meandering Main Street.

Wes Mitchel had told them Hangtown was the biggest camp in the Mother Lode, since it was so close to where Marshall had discovered the precious metal. Even from this distance, they could see a church, and what looked like a meeting hall or theater, along with other buildings that could be hotels or restaurants.

Men were digging all over the hillsides. Most had their cabins close by. Some were even plying their shovels right in the middle of Main Street!

"Yes!" whispered Edward, pumping his arm.

Richard's eyes shone. Lewis' grin spread from ear to ear.

Suddenly they no longer felt exhausted.

Their enthusiasm soon spread to the others. Handshakes. Back slaps.

"We made it!"

"We're here!

"Let's get that gold!"

Pulling into town, Edward felt uncertain. "Where do we go? What do we do? Where can we sleep? Set up housekeeping? Stake a claim?"

Snowshoe laughed. "I'll point you in the right direction. After that, it's up to you."

Others of the wagon train were discussing whether to stay in Hangtown or go on to other camps up and down the Mother Lode. Hopefully places where others hadn't mined out all the gold.

"Look Momma!" Ellen pointed. "There's the hanging tree Mister Snowshoe Thompson told us about. Right there in back of the Jackass Inn."

"Ellen! Watch your language."

"Well, that's what the sign says."

On their first night in the Sierras, sitting around a campfire, Snowshoe had told them about the unusual name for the town.

"California's been an independent republic since Mexico lost the war, Snowshoe had said. "So, until it becomes a state, the citizens hand out justice anyway they see fit."

"They hang them?" asked an incredulous Richard.

"Hasn't happened often. Hardly more'n half a dozen have graced the hanging tree. It's mostly a real peaceable place…"

❊ ❊ ❊

"What do you think, Caroline?" Edward asked now, as he helped her down from the wagon seat. "Does this look like a place you could set up housekeeping?"

She looked around in bewilderment, shaking her head. "This is no place to bring up a child." She frowned. "Even if there are some substantial buildings, the town looks like a pig sty—if you ask me.

"All that trash. Boots and shirts, empty tins and bottles, worn-out pots and kettles. You'd think they could at least pick up after themselves."

"They're too busy." Edward smiled. "They're digging gold. Getting rich. Like I'm going to do—starting tomorrow."

"Well, you do what you have to do. Ellen and I are going on to someplace where women can make an honest living."

Ellen pouted, clearly entranced with the bustle of activity around her.

"You need to go to school," her mother admonished.

"You can teach me."

"I've got to make a living for the two of us."

Caroline hugged Ellen to her side. "I'm thinking of going with some of the others. To Sacramento. A bigger city will have decent schools. And actual houses, with porches and vegetable gardens."

She turned to her daughter. "What do you think, pumpkin? Wouldn't a real house be nice?"

Ellen looked down, shoulders slumped, avoiding her mother's eyes. "I guess so."

Edward felt a sinking sensation. *What if Ellen expects me to go to Sacramento with them?*

"Are you going to be all right, going to Sacramento with your mother?"

He held his breath.

Ellen looked around. Then at him.

She stood taller.

"We'll be fine. I'm not so little any more." She paused. "I walked all the way here. I can take care of myself, now."

"I know you can." Edward sighed in relief.

"And, Sacramento's not that far away." He touched her shoulder. "We can write each other. I'm sure mail and packages go back and forth nearly every day."

Caroline smiled. "Of course we can. We can even visit, once in a while."

She turned to Edward. Took his hand. "Thank you for your help."

Edward looked down suddenly shy. "I should be thanking you. For your friendship."

"Ellen," her mother admonished, "thank Mr. Daingerfield for taking such good care of us all the way across the country."

Ellen smiled. She gave a nice curtsey. "Thank you Mr. Daingerfield. You were my best friend on the whole trip."

A lump clogged his throat, as he watched Caroline and Ellen climb back on the wagon to continue their journey.

"Write, and let me know how you're getting along," he called out, as they followed the wagons ahead of them.

"We will. Come visit when we all get settled."

"I will."

I feel like I'm losing part of my family.

Chapter Twenty-Eight

Dear Family, Edward wrote. *We're finally here! In Hangtown, California. While it's too big to be called a 'camp' as most of the settlements around here are, to me it looks too disorganized to be called a 'town'. (Leastwise, not like any town in Indiana.)*

Hangtown has one Main Street, squiggling down the center of a narrow valley, surrounded by foothills that lead to the high country of the Sierra Nevada Range to the east. That's the only real road, the rest being trails to other business establishments, mining claims, and homes, shacks, or tents.

The three of us purchased a house and mining claim from a couple of brothers. One wanted to go to San Francisco, and the other decided to return to his home in Pennsylvania. We paid $710 dollars for it. Fortunately, we got a good price for our oxen. Even after all the hard work and little food or water towards the end, they were still amazingly strong and healthy.

The house isn't all that grand, being built of logs and having four rooms: kitchen, and three bedrooms. It's pretty rough, not much furniture. In fact we broke up the wagon to make a table and two benches for the kitchen. But, it's better than a tent, which lots of men live in, and plenty good enough for us. Like everyone else, we're too busy mining gold to pay attention to fixing up the house.

You can write me here. We have a post office. (So you see we really are almost a town.) I have no idea how long it will take for letters to get to Greencastle and back, but just address yours to E.B. Daingerfield, Hangtown, California, and I'll get it just fine.

Next letter, I'll tell you more. I'm too tired tonight. This mining is hard work...

* * *

Edward stopped digging and wiped his face. The blazing sun beat down on the three of them. He looked around. All up and down the hillside, groups of men were doing exactly what he was—digging dry earth out of holes about six feet square and five or six feet deep.

The original course of the creek was completely obliterated, its water being distributed into numberless little ditches, and conducted to the miners through canvas hoses, looking like immensely long slimy sea serpents.

"Any gold yet?" asked Edward, looking up from the hole.

Richard paused in shoveling the dirt Edward had tossed up, onto a sluice called a Long Tom, and looked expectantly at Lewis. He was washing mud off of any gold there might be. Water from the canvas hose flowed into the shallow trough of boards, about fifteen feet long by fifteen inches wide. Lewis picked out stones, and let the dirt fall through a sieve. The water washed out the mud, separating gold nuggets or dust in the ripple box under the end of the Long Tom.

Lewis, spattered with mud from head to foot, peered into the ripple box, and shook his head.

"Nope. Not yet." He looked at the pile of mud they'd collected that day. "We haven't had much of anything and we've been at it four whole days."

"I guess we just keep digging." Richard tossed another shovel-full into the Long Tom.

Edward continued digging dirt out of the hole. Tomorrow they'd rotate, and he'd be working water through the Long Tom, hoping to find gold. So far, they only had a dusting of powder to show for their work.

Edward mentally tallied their food bill at Mark Hopkin's grocery. Five pounds of sugar, $1.25; ten pounds of beef, $2.50; fifty pounds of flour, $6.00; seven pounds of pork, $1.40; two pounds of coffee, $1.00. Over twelve dollars they owed the store! Plus five dollars for a new pick handle.

"Come on gold," he pleaded, "be there!"

As the shadows lengthened, Edward climbed out of his hole. Tomorrow Richard would start a new one right next to it, hoping to find a vein of gold they could follow.

Lewis redirected the canvas hose to let the water flow down the dry gulch.

Richard stacked his shovel next to Edward's.

"We've got it!" shouted Lewis. "Look here!" He pointed to the Long Tom's box. "Gold!"

The three of them looked at the coating of powder and small pile of granules. Probably wasn't worth more than a couple of dollars, but real gold, nonetheless.

Richard grabbed Edward. Lewis joined in, all dancing a jig.

* * *

They were carefully scraping up the smattering of gold in the Long Tom box the next day, when word reached them. It had spread through town and up the hills, from one claim to the next, as if blown on the hot, dry September wind. "Bull and bear fight. Main Street. Tomorrow."

Ben Nickerson, owner of the Union Hotel was promoting the fight, taking a small percentage of all money bet on the outcome.

Men came from camps all around. They lined the street, perched on roofs, and hung out of every second story window. Edward caught their excitement as someone might catch another person's cold.

"What are you wagering, young man?" asked a gray-whiskered miner.

"You... you mean betting?" stammered Edward.

"Yup. Place your bet. Bull or the bear? Winners divvy up the losers' gold."

Edward pondered. He had some gold powder and flakes in the pouch around his neck. Not a whole lot. Not even enough to pay off his share of what they owed the store, and buy the next week's supplies.

A cheer went up as two *vaqueros* herded a handsome bull into the arena set aside for the fight in the middle of Main Street. Men cheered and Edward felt a surge of admiration for the animal.

Muscles rippled as it moved with dignity out into the open center of the street. He held his head high, dark eyes glaring at the crowd. Magnificent long, pointed horns challenged anyone or anything to take him on. The bull pawed the dirt with hard hooves, and then lowered his head, pointing its horns first this way, then that.

Next, another two men rolled in an iron cage on wheels. It must at one time have carried lions and tigers for a circus. They positioned it as far from the bull as possible. Inside, a huge brown bear growled and snarled.

A stab of fear swept through Edward, raising the hairs on his arms at the sight.

Which would be more likely to win in a fight to the death?

"Place a bet?" asked the old miner again.

"I... I haven't decided yet."

Edward looked around for Richard and Lewis. The crowd had swallowed them up.

"Make up your mind. Once they start, it's too late to wager," said the miner.

A long, heavy chain trailed from a collar around the bear's neck, out between the bars, and onto the dirt. One of the men grabbed the far end of the chain. The other put a metal spike through the last ring, and drove the stake into the street with a large mallet. The two men opened the cage door, and then leapt over the barricade protecting the onlookers from both animals.

Should I bet? Or not? Edward asked himself. What are Richard and Lewis doing? If I'm going to bet, it has to be now. I wish I knew if they were betting.

The bear lunged and stumbled out onto the dirt street. Instinctively, the crowd nearest the bear stepped back with a collective gasp.

As the bear lumbered slowly, awkwardly around in a circle, sniffing the air and growling, Edward made up his mind.

"I'll place my bet on the bull!" he called out to the miner. "With his strength and horns, nothing can beat him."

When all the bets had been placed and recorded, the signal was given to start the fight. The *vaqueros* prodded the bull into the center of the arena, and then leapt over the barricade.

The bear pulled at the chain, tightening the collar around his neck. Backing up, he suddenly rose on his hind feet, pawed the air with long front claws, and sniffed as though blind but scenting the adversary.

Just then the bull charged, bringing the full weight of his head against the bear's side, tearing a huge gash with one of his horns.

Edward roared along with the rest of the crowd. "Yes! My bet is safe."

The bear howled. Then, with a suddenness that belied sight, he tucked into a somersault, ripping the tender undercarriage of the bull's stomach with his sharp claws.

Now both animals were bleeding profusely. The bull hobbled to safety, beyond reach of the bear's chain. Sides heaving, head lowered, the bull wanted nothing more to do with the wild thing opposite him.

Edward felt for both of them. While all those around him yelled and jeered, he shook his head.

Suddenly Richard was next to him.

"These animals are suffering." Edward had to shout to be heard over the roar of the crowd. "For what? Entertainment?"

"Well," Richard yelled back, "what did you expect?"

"I don't know. I guess I didn't even think about it."

The crowd yelled and chanted. "Fight! Fight!"

The *Vaqueros* risked life and limb prodding the bull to within reach of the bear.

Although bleeding, the bear reared up on his hind legs again. With precision timing, the bull lowered his head and charged the bear, knocking it down and goring its other side.

From the ground, the bear grabbed the bull's nose in its teeth, hanging on for dear life.

The bull's horns were useless in this maneuver. He kicked with his sharp hooves, but to no effect.

The bear finally released the dying bull.

A moment of silence fell over the crowd. Then cheers for the contestants rose all along the dusty street. Joy for those who had bet on the winner. A wry smile and shrug of the shoulders from those whose gold had been on the loser.

A strange feeling of emptiness overcame Edward. He'd gambled money he didn't have to spare. Suddenly the thought of the gold he might have won in the bet felt like Judas Iscariot's thirty pieces of silver.

Two senseless animals suffered pain. One died.

Edward knew he could acquire more money—mine it, or get other jobs and earn it. But, no matter how long he lived, he would *never* forget the bull and bear fight on Main Street in Hangtown.

Chapter Twenty-Nine

"Oh my gosh! Come quick!"

Edward stared. Blinked his eyes, to make sure what he was seeing was really there.

"What?" shouted Richard, as Lewis scrambling out of the ditch and over the pile of dirt and mud.

"There," said Edward, pointing to the ripple box of the Long Tom. "Is that what I think it is?"

All three men stood stock-still, eyes bulging, mouths agape.

Richard shook his head in wonder. "It sure looks like gold to me."

Lewis nodded in agreement. "*Lots* of gold."

"I'm not seeing things?" Edward asked. "I'm not crazy?"

There in the ripple box lay, not a dusting, but pieces, nuggets and chunks of gold, shining in reflected sunlight, just waiting to be picked up by eager, trembling fingers.

"We... we're... we're rich!" Edward's voice rose from a whisper to a shout, finally allowing himself to believe his eyes. "That's more gold than I've ever *seen* in one place."

* * *

After their discovery, the days weren't long enough. They berated the fact the sun came up later and set earlier each day as September slid relentlessly toward October.

At first light they rushed to their claim, began digging, following the vein of gold as it led first straight ahead, then to the left, sometimes going deeper, then upward, nearer the surface, before dropping deeper again. They barely took time to eat, so excited were they with the treasure God had seemingly dropped into their hands.

On the first Saturday after discovering gold, instead of heating water in pails on the stove and bathing in the laundry tub, they took clean clothes with them and headed to the bathhouse in town.

"This is going to be so much easier than pumping bucket after bucket of water to heat on the stove—enough for each of us to fill the metal bathtub and take a bath," Lewis said with a grin.

""And then pumping and heating more water to wash our clothes in," Richard agreed.

Edward could hardly wait.

Once at the bathhouse, they weighed out three dollars worth of gold each and waited in line, clean towel and bar of soap in hand. Three men stood in line ahead of them, and more arrived as they waited. Most all the men left their claims on Saturday to come to town, to do errands and buy food and supplies for the coming week. Edward visited casually with the man behind him, feeling smug he had the gold to splurge on a commercial bath.

At last his number was called. As instructed, he walked down the hall, fitted his key into the lock on the door, and entered a small room with a large tub of steaming-hot water. Carefully laying his clean clothes on a shelf, he took off his muddy boots and put them outside the door. Then, peeling off his dirty clothes, he left them in a heap on the floor and stepped into the deliciously warm water.

By the time he'd soaped up, the water in the tub was a murky brown. He pulled a bell cord attached to the tub, and moments later a male assistant came in—Edward's cleaned boots in hand—to pour clean warm water from a bucket, over his soapy hair and body.

Afterwards, he joined Richard and Lewis to have barber Doc Johnson, one of the very few black people in Hangtown, trim their squeaky-clean hair and beards. Looking in the mirror Johnson held for him, Edward was amazed at the difference in his appearance. They'd not had the opportunity to get haircuts since leaving home last mid-April—five whole months ago! Now, his light brown hair just brushed the collar of his clean shirt. His short beard outlined his face, accentuating his blue eyes, and making him look mature.

Feeling like entirely new and different people, they walked, taking their filthy dirty clothes with them, to the laundry on Quartz Alley in the Chinatown area.

"Putee names on bags, prease," said the man at the counter, in a singsong voice as he handed them each a large bag for their laundry. "Be ready in morning."

"That sure beats boiling them in our own tub and hanging them out to dry on the line next to the house," commented Richard.

"All three of us are washed and our laundry disposed of, in less than half the time it takes for one bath at home," agreed Lewis.

"It never really occurred to me, how much easier life is with money!" added Edward, smiling and cocking his head.

"Now," he added, "let's go pay our bill at the store and shop for food for next week."

"Yes!" the others agreed. "Hopkins, will be glad to see us walk in *this* time!"

They made their way to the mercantile, tipping their hats to those they passed on the way. Carts and carriages drove up and down the main street, turning up dust.

The bell rang as they opened the door to the store. After settling their outstanding bill with Hopkins, they began looking around.

"Cut some of that beef into steaks," requested Edward, "and I'd like a couple dozen fresh eggs, and some of those green beans and a dozen ears of corn."

One of the boys working for Mark Hopkins packed what they'd ordered into boxes, which they carried back to the house.

"Now, what'll we do?" asked Lewis as they stashed food away.

"What would you like me to cook for dinner?" responded Edward, looking forward to having so much fresh food to work with.

"I think..." mused Richard, "I think we should celebrate by going out. What do you think about dinner at the Carey House?"

"Great idea!" agreed Lewis. "Maybe we could have that Hangtown Fry I've heard so much about."

In no time at all, they had joined other diners at a long table, wooden benches on each side. "What's a Hangtown Fry?" asked Richard.

"The dish was first made, right here," explained Pete, the owner, "One day a miner plunked down his poke full of gold on the counter and demanded the best meal in town. The costliest items we had were eggs, bacon, and canned eastern oysters.

"Cook combined those ingredients—three eastern oysters, two strips of bacon and two large eggs—to make an omelet. It was an immediate success, and became known as Hangtown Fry."

"We'd all three like Hangtown Fries," Edward ordered.

"You'll like 'em," said a customer seated across the table. "The best restaurants in San Francisco are now serving Hangtown Fry to visiting miners.

"By the way, name's George," he said, standing up to shake hands.

After discussing the weather and mining prospects, George asked what they thought about the names being suggested for Hangtown.

"They're changing the name of the town?" asked Edward. "First I've heard of it."

"Yep," said George. "Seems we're gettin' too gentrified for a hangin' name."

"Well, we'll be part of the United States any day now," added Pete. "Folks around here want a more dignified name, for listing in the U. S. register."

"So what's being suggested?" asked Richard.

"Dry Diggin's, for one," said George. "On account that's what makes Hangtown different from other towns. Most of 'em are just mined along the rivers and streams, but here we dig every which place."

"Actually," added Pete, who seemed to be an authority on local history, "Dry Diggings was the original name of the camp a couple of years ago. Then on January 22, 1849, three men were hanged on Main Street for stealing. This was the first known lynching in the Mother Lode, so Dry Diggings became known as Hangtown."

"Another likely name's Placerville," said George, "'for the deposits of gold, glaciers dumped here thousands of years ago. Since we mine gold where we find it, instead of just along the rivers, our method of mining is called 'placer' mining."

"Well," commented Edward, "Dry Diggings is more descriptive, but Placerville sounds more progressive."

"My cousin Edward, here," Richard explained, "writes for the newspaper back home in Indiana. He's an expert on words."

After the meal, which they all agreed was, 'different, but I wouldn't want to eat it every day,' they decided to walk around Hangtown—or Dry Diggings, or Placerville—whatever it ended up being called.

They walked along the narrow, dusty street, noticing that nearly every other building was a saloon.

"Let's go see what they're doing," said Lewis, eyes shining.

Edward had his doubts, remembering his bet on the bull and bear fight. He'd worked too hard for his gold to lose it in a card game, though a whisky would go down real smooth after their meal.

It took a few minutes for their eyes to adjust, when they entered the dim room. The six tables had miners playing all sorts of card games, each table loaded with piles of gold and silver. Edward instinctively reached for his own poke, hanging around his neck, under his shirt.

A piano player in the corner added a tuneful background to the clink of silver, the spinning of a roulette wheel, and the shuffling of cards.

The three sauntered over to the bar and ordered drinks. They watched the games for a few minutes, none of them inclined to join in.

Before long, three young 'ladies' joined them. Rose took Edward by the arm and started a conversation. He noticed how pretty she was, all soft golden curls, blue eyes, ruby cheeks framed in lace and ruffles.

"Come on, handsome," Rose coaxed. "I bet those big strong muscles could use a massage." She ran her fingers up his arm, sending a ripple of reaction from stem to stern. *Especially* stern.

Edward had no doubts what the 'massage' would turn into. Even in Greencastle there were places 'nicer folks' wouldn't go. He'd never been to one, but if he had, his folks would have known about it before he even got home.

I'm not in Greencastle, he thought, and no one at home will ever know what I'm up to here.

He smiled at Rose. She was more pretty than beautiful, but that just suited his mood on this sunny Saturday afternoon.

By the time he let her lead him upstairs, he realized neither Richard nor Lewis were still standing at the bar.

Heart thumping, he left the sound of piano and card games behind. Climbing the stairs, he had a fleeting thought of Susanna. It amazed him to realize how seldom he had thought about her since leaving home.

Just now, he couldn't even picture her face!

Chapter Thirty

That night, Edward sat at the kitchen table, writing an article for *The Argus* by the light of a flickering lantern. He recounted their gold discovery, describing the softly rounded nuggets that winked and gleamed from the ripple box. He detailed their day on the town from beginning to... well he stopped short of writing about the saloon and what had transpired there.

He thought about writing up the bull and bear fight, but discarded the idea. He knew the gentle folks in Greencastle would be aghast at the idea of such barbarian entertainment. And he had difficulty admitting he'd wagered money he couldn't afford at the time, on the outcome.

Sitting back, Edward realized this was the first article he'd written since leaving Fort Laramie on—he thumbed through his journal—*June 24*. And now it was September sixteenth. This Friday would mark one whole month they'd been in Hangtown!

Time was a funny thing, he mused. Parts of the overland crossing, especially days and nights crossing the desert and Humboldt Sink, seemed to have taken forever. Much of the rest of the journey had passed in an instant, filled with beauty and abundance.

No matter what Rag Town postmaster Mitchell had predicted, Edward still wasn't anywhere near being able to relive those horrible days and nights from Sublett's Cut-Off to the Humboldt Sink.

Not even for a story and byline in *The Argus.*

He'd sent a letter home when they first arrived in Hangtown. For all he knew, it was still waiting in the Rag Town Post Office to be picked up by an authorized carrier going east. No need to write again so soon. Besides, when they read the article in the *Argus,* they'd know everything he might have written them.

What about Susanna? He'd not written her at all.

He remembered the day he'd left Greencastle...

❊ ❊ ❊

April 10, 1850. Edward had been up since before dawn—alternating between excitement for the adventure ahead, and a deep sense of finality—when he realized he wouldn't see any of his family, friends, all he was familiar with, for at least two or three years... If ever.

Mother hid her misgivings as she packed slices of ham and biscuits, for them to eat on their way to St. Louis.

"Did you remember your extra boots?" she asked.

"Yes, I packed them in one of the mule's saddle bags last night."

She kissed him, and gave him a hug. But, while he empathized with her love and sense of loss, he was anxious now to be underway on the adventure of his life.

As they mounted their horses, Elizabeth stood beside Lewis. Shyly she handed him an envelope. "It's a letter. Read it every night and remember me. Our promise." She blushed. "And a lock of my hair for luck."

Possibly emboldened by Elizabeth, Susanna came to Edward, and untying the blue ribbon in her hair, she made a bow of it around his arm. He leaned down and kissed her cheek.

"Godspeed, E.B." she said.

"Thank you," he whispered, feeling a bit embarrassed, with everyone looking on.

A moment later, sitting tall in the saddle, Edward felt like Sir Lancelot going off to seek the Holy Grail.

As the three young men and Edward's father clucked their horses and two pack mules into motion, his twelve-year-old brother, Lawrence, trotted along, holding on to Edward's stirrup.

Lawrence had argued for weeks about going to California with them. Now, panting, he said, "By the time I get 'old enough' there won't be any adventures *left.* Can't I at least go with you to see the Mississippi River? I could help Father bring the animals back."

Edward looked down into blue, pleading eyes. If their positions were reversed, *he'd* be begging, just like his little brother. His face softened into a smile as he kicked his foot out of the stirrup to give Lawrence a toehold. Then he held out an arm.

With a grin, Lawrence grabbed the offered arm and vaulted onto the horse.

"You promise to come back home with Father when we reach the Mississippi? No begging!" Lawrence put his arms around Edward's waist. He could feel his brother's heart pounding against his back.

"I promise!"

"You'd better. Or else I'll tell Father to make you walk all the way home—by yourself!"

Soon, children of all ages joined the small parade as they traveled the dirt streets of Greencastle. Adults, too, waved goodbye and called out, "Godspeed!"

"How long will it take, do you think? To get to the Mississippi? Well, to California, too? What will you eat? Will you see Indians?"

On and on the questions flew.

Edward knew he would treasure this ride with his brother for the rest of his life. With a ten-year difference in ages, they'd never spent much time together. Never attended the same schools or shared the same friends. Aside from family meals, they'd each gone their own ways. They even had different bedrooms...

* * *

Edward stretched and yawned hugely. The lantern sputtered, his eyes felt scratchy. He looked at the neat stack of pages on the table before him.

He wondered how he'd gone from writing about hitting a vein of gold and the aftermath day on the town—to Lawrence. He went back through his thoughts, like Mother unraveling a too-small sweater and carefully winding the yarn into a ball for some other project.

Lawrence. Leaving home. Susanna. That's it! He'd felt guilty about not writing her since he'd left home.

He still had the blue ribbon, folded in the box where he kept his clean socks.

Every time he came across it, the ribbon seemed more a reproach than a symbol of everlasting love.

Chapter Thirty-One

Nearly a month later, Edward wrote another article for *The Argus.* "Today, Saturday, October 26," he wrote, "was an historic date for the three of us, here in California..."

On that date a United States Census taker came to Placerville, and California statehood became real to Edward.

Agent Andrew Coffenburg wrote their names and data as the eighteenth 'family' (residents sharing a domicile) on the page. He first listed Lewis H. Rudesill, as age 22, male. Occupation: miner. Value of real estate owned: $710. Born in Indiana.

The spaces for "Married within the year" and "Attending school" were both left unchecked.

Coffenburg then looked enquiringly at Edward. "Edwin B. Daingerfield," he answered. "Age 22. Born in Virginia. I'm a miner, also."

His head whirled. Our town's name is now officially 'Placerville' and my name is on the first United States census ever taken in the state of California!

When the agent turned to Richard, he responded, "Richard W. Chenowith, age 27. Born in Virginia. Occupation: miner, as well."

The agent packed up his papers, ink and pen, and turned to shake their hands. "Congratulations, you are now registered as among the first citizens of the State of California.

"Although Congress admitted California as the thirty-first state in the Union on September ninth," the agent said, "October twenty-ninth this year, has been designated as the day to celebrate California's admission into the Union."

"Yes, sir," Edward answered. "We heard that a few days ago. In fact, we're all planning to go to Sacramento to see the celebration."

Chapter Thirty-Two

Early on October 29, the three of them, all cleaned up and dressed in their city clothes, joined several other miners riding horses, mules, and wagons to Sacramento. Edward had written back and forth to Caroline Gould, and they were planning to celebrate the day together.

"Land's sake! See what the cat dragged in," Caroline exclaimed as she opened the door to her two-story boarding house. "Come in, come in."

"I'm impressed," Edward said, wiping the dust off his boots on the doormat. "You really own all this?"

"Well, it's not completely paid for," Caroline answered, blushing in pride. "But it's all mine, as long as I pay the mortgage on time."

"How big is it?" asked Richard.

"Four bedrooms upstairs, one down. I have the downstairs—parlor, dining room, kitchen, and bedroom. I've got eight boarders, two to a room upstairs.

"You'll meet them when they come home for dinner at noon. After that I'll make us a cold supper to take to the park on the bank of the American River. Speeches, picnic, and fireworks afterwards."

Edward looked around, nodding approval. “Ah, where’s Ellen?”

“In boarding school. This is a great place for me to make a good living, but not to raise a young daughter.”

At Edward’s look of disappointment, Caroline continued, “She and the other girls will meet us at the park, so you’ll see her there.”

Lewis and Edward looked toward Richard, their spokesman. He, standing straighter, said in a clear voice that gave evidence he’d rehearsed the words, “Ma’am, if your husband had survived, he’d have dug enough gold to make your life more secure. But, since he didn’t… we’d like to give you some of what we’ve discovered.”

Richard held out a small leather pouch. Caroline opened the drawstring. Inside, three good-sized nuggets lay nestled together, bright as a smile.

“Oh… Oh my goodness!” Caroline gasped. “Why… I can’t possibly…”

“Yes you can,” Edward took over. “We want you to have it. Gould would want you to have it. Use the gold to help pay off the mortgage on your house.”

“But,” Caroline shook her head, at a loss for words. “I’ve never had friends such as you three.”

She paused. “Thank you.”

One at a time, she held Richard’s, then Lewis’, and finally, Edward’s, hand in hers. “Thank each of you, from the bottom of my heart.”

Friendship. Edward pondered the word.

Of the three of them, he understood he and Caroline had the deepest friendship. Lewis was somewhat impatient. Driven to find as much gold as possible, so he could go home and marry Elizabeth. Richard could be seen as standoffish. But, while he wasn't naturally warm and outgoing, he *was* steady, loyal, and a natural leader.

But, Edward and Caroline had a rare kinship. Which, when one thought about it, was strange. Caroline, at least ten years his senior, had married and buried two husbands. And raised a ten-year-old daughter, virtually on her own. And now, she had her own boarding house, which she ran almost single-handedly, and very capably.

What did she see in him? Fresh out of university (hadn't finished, at that) he'd done nothing in life. Not even, he finally admitted to himself, fallen in love. Ever.

Not long afterward, Edward and the others enjoyed sharing dinner with Caroline's boarders, a convivial group made up mostly of merchants and skilled craftsmen. Edward learned Caroline had a girl who worked two days a week, helping with laundry and cleaning, as well as a one-day-a-week handyman for gardening and never-ending repairs and maintenance.

Later that afternoon, they joined the throng of people all heading for the park. They walked in groups of twos and threes, mostly men, but some families, all carrying blankets, picnic baskets, and wraps. Although the air was only gently crisp, it would be cool as soon as the sun went down.

A bandstand had been erected on a bluff overlooking the American River. The musicians were setting up, with riffs on the drums, toots of trumpets, and trills on a piccolo.

"Mamma!" called Ellen as she ran up with two other girls her age.

"Look who's here," said Caroline, turning Ellen around.

At the sight of Edward, she blushed, and turned suddenly shy.

"Introduce your friends," reminded her mother.

She took her friends by the hands and led them to Edward, smiling. "Mr. Daingerfield, these are my friends, Mary Kate and Polly."

Edward took the proffered hands into his own large, work-roughened one. "Mary Kate. Polly. It's a pleasure to meet you."

He was about to ask Ellen about school—what she was learning, who her favorite teachers were—when she gave him another wide, excited smile, and scampered off, her two giggling friends trailing behind her.

"She's been so thrilled to finally see you again, she's talked of nothing else. And now she's turned shy. I don't understand it," her mother complained.

"When we were part of a wagon train, we were together constantly," Edward murmured. "Being friends was natural. But now she's in school, in a different setting, with ten-year-old schoolmates."

He understood it. But nonetheless, he felt a bit deflated. Ellen wasn't the only one who had been looking forward to their seeing each other again.

The band started playing a sprightly march. Edward's disappointment vanished as everyone began clapping in time to the music. Soon, men carrying brand new flags featuring thirty-one stars in a field of blue came marching by. Others joined the parade circling the bandstand.

When the music came to an end, a man dressed in a black broadcloth suit and bow tie stepped up to address the crowd.

"Ladies and gentlemen," he shouted into a megaphone, "boys and girls, we are met on this most auspicious occasion to celebrate entrance into statehood, of this, the far-westerly-most state. The golden state of California!"

Cheering erupted as everyone stood, clapping hands.

"President Zachary Taylor, former general and hero of the Battle of Buena Vista, supported our immediate admittance into the Union, especially after gold was discovered and so many people immigrated here."

Edward, Richard, Lewis and Caroline pointed to each other. *People like you and me,* they mouthed, nodding and smiling.

"But, national politics clouded the future of California statehood. The issue of balancing states that permitted slavery and those that did not, was a factor. And concern for other areas conceded to the United States by Mexico—Utah, New Mexico, and its boundary with Texas."

At the mention of slavery, Edward felt a shiver run up his neck. His roots were in Virginia. His ancestors had been slaveholders.

"I was born in Virginia," he whispered to Ellen. "My family has had slaves there since the 1630's. It's not a good system, but it's the only economically feasible solution to the cost of raising tobacco.

"I expect one of the reasons my parents moved to Indiana, was because of the slavery issue. But then, they don't grow tobacco in Indiana."

Caroline, on the other side of her daughter, smiled in understanding. They turned their attention to the speaker.

"In 1845 Texas was admitted to the Union as a slave state. Most Southerners wanted all of the territory acquired from Mexico to permit slavery. Northerners opposed this. In fact some Northerners are advocating abolition of slavery in all parts of the union.

"Senator Henry Clay proposed a compromise that would address these issues, early this year. But President Taylor, while advocating immediate statehood for California, opposed the Clay compromise.

"As most of you know, President Taylor died from typhoid fever on July 9..."

"I didn't know that," whispered Edward. All the others shrugged their shoulders and agreed. Where had they been on July 9? Independence Rock... Devil's Gate... crossing Sweetwater River over and over...?

"Vice President Millard Fillmore became president and supported the Clay Compromise, along with senators Daniel Webster and Stephen Douglas.

"On August first of this year, the Senate passed the Utah Bill. Although hotly debated, the California Admission Bill passed the Senate on August thirteenth. The House of Representatives took up the Texas—New Mexico Boundary Bill on August twenty-eighth, passing it on September sixth.

"With Clay, Fillmore, Webster, and Douglas supporting it, California became the thirty-first state (non-slave) on September 9, 1850."

Everyone stood and cheered. Men threw their hats in the air. Edward's heart swelled when he felt Ellen's small hand burrow into his. It made him feel part of a family, with an additional, much-younger sibling.

The band struck up *The Star Spangled Banner*. Everyone stood, hats off, hands over hearts, and joined in:

Oh say can you see, by the dawn's early light...

Soon the music became more raucous.

The notes to the popular song, *Sacramento,* filled the evening air. And soon all were chiming in on the chorus:

Then blow ye winds, hi-oh,
For Cal-i-for-ny-o!
There's plenty of gold, so I've been told,
On the banks of the Sacramento.

As Caroline dished up her supper of cold chicken, potato salad, and biscuits, still slightly warm from the oven, Edward purchased hot apple cider, bought by the cup, from a vendor with a kettle over a fire.

"This is delicious," Edward remarked, licking his fingers.

"I envy your boarders," Lewis commented, helping himself to another biscuit.

As the sun set in the west, the water of the American River turned into a ribbon of flame.

The sky darkened and stars pulsated. The first of the fireworks shot upwards.

"Ohhhh."

"Ahhhh."

"Look at the colors!"

As the brilliant sparks of light—and their reflections in the American River—filled the night, Edward felt a deep sigh of contentment fill his chest.

He was an American, living in the newest state in the American Union, surrounded by good friends...

Could *anything* be better than this?

Chapter Thirty-Three

"I don't believe this!" Edward scratched his head and peered into the ripple box. "There's nothing here. We've been putting dirt through here all day, and *we don't have any gold!"*

"Let me see." Richard pushed Edward aside and looked. "Well I'll be damned! He's right."

Lewis clambered out of the deep hole he'd dug. "But, how can that be?"

"The vein we've been following must have turned, or gone deeper… or something," Richard said.

"Or run out." Edward felt a clutch of fear tighten his stomach. "What if it's gone?"

Lewis slapped his shoulder. "Tomorrow, we'll back up and see if we can find out where the vein went. If we can't latch on to it, we'll just start digging new holes until we find another one." He swept an arm. "There's gold all over these hills. Just look where men are digging. We'll find more. Just you see."

Edward kept silent, but felt a nagging apprehension.

⁂

Some time that night, the rain started. They awoke to a gray day, wisps of clouds caught like cotton in the tops of the trees, the mountains beyond, obscured.

The rain continued all day. Not a storm—all thunder and lightning, with torrents of heavy rain drops washing away everything in their path. Just a light, steady flow.

Not like Indiana, thought Edward, *where a downpour sweeps in, dumps its load, and then moves on.*

When the three went out to survey their claim, the hole Lewis had dug yesterday—the one with no gold in it—was filled with muddy water.

They looked around. A few men were making half-hearted attempts to dig, but most were staying inside. Staying dry.

Richard gave voice to what all of them were thinking. "We might as well wait it out in the cabin. It's bound to be clear tomorrow. We'll decide what to do then."

But, the next day was even worse than the one before. The rain had increased. Rivulets ran down the normally dry hills, tumbling pebbles in their wake.

The three retreated into the cabin once again. It smelled of unwashed bodies and wet wool.

Edward shivered. "Fire's almost out. I'll get more wood."

When he returned, he was shaking his head in disbelief. "These three logs are all that's left of our wood pile, and *they're all wet.*"

"So, go out and chop more." Lewis clomped into his room and slammed the door.

Edward stomped over and opened it. "I do all the cooking and most of the cleaning up around here. The least you and Richard could do is see we have logs for the fire!"

"You're right," Richard conceded. "But, there's nothing we can do until the rain stops. Then all three of us will work together to cut down a tree, drag it back, and chop it up for firewood. And, now we'll know to keep some of the wood in the kitchen to stay dry."

"Meanwhile, what'll we eat?' asked Lewis.

"A cold meal today," answered Edward, "and if it's still raining tomorrow, we'll have to put on our slickers and walk into town for dinner."

As the temperature dropped, they added extra shirts, jackets, and finally, wrapped up in blankets, as well.

"What're you doing?" asked Richard, standing at the kitchen table, peering over Edward's shoulder.

"Writing another article for *The Argus*," answered Edward. "Telling them about the statehood celebration."

Richard smiled. "That was something to behold."

"What if we don't find any more gold?" asked Edward.

"We will. We're sure to."

"But... I've been thinking. Maybe one of us should find steady employment."

"Why?"

"Just so we'd have reliable income. Something we could count on. To pay for our food, at least."

Exciting as the discovery of a gold vein had been, Edward felt pulled to do something other than the frenzied clawing for gold they'd been doing ever since they arrived. He actually envied the gentlemen he'd seen in Placerville, dressed in clean clothes, running nice establishments, taking hard-won gold from the miners in exchange for goods and services.

"I don't think Lewis would go for it," Richard replied. "We came to California for the gold. And besides, we've got plenty from when the pickings were good. We could eat all winter off what we've already got, and still have time to find more before we had to start back home."

"When do you suppose we'll do that?"

"Go home?" Richard paused. "I've been thinking we could keep mining—as much as possible—this winter and spring, then through June. It took about four months to get here, so if we left early July, we'd be home by late October. Before the snow came."

"Home." A warm sense of nostalgia filled Edward. Then he shuddered. "But, I don't look forward to going back across that God-awful desert."

"Me neither," agreed Richard.

The next day, the rain finally stopped, but the ground was too saturated to dig for gold. Or to tramp through the forest to try chopping down a waterlogged tree.

❊ ❊ ❊

"I'm going to see if I can find regular work," Edward announced, as they got up from breakfast at the Carey House.

"Why, in the world would you do that?" asked Lewis.

"Because I *feel* like it," Edward said grumpily, unwilling to discuss his decision.

“Well, if you think you’re going to get a cushy, soft job and still share in the gold Richard and I bust our backs digging,” Lewis stormed, “you’ve got another think a-coming.”

“Besides,” Richard chimed in, “what kind of employment could you get here?”

“Yeah! You’re going to be a bar tender? Play the honky-tonk piano? Or maybe you’re going to pull your eyes slanty and take in laundry.”

“Maybe I’ll become a cook.” Edward looked back towards the kitchen.

“They’ve already got a cook,” Lewis spat out.

“And besides,” Richard predicted, “as soon as the weather gets better and we strike it rich, you’re going to want to quit the job and come back to mining with us.

“You don’t want to promise to do a job,” he added, quietly, “and then quit when it suits you. That’s not fair to the guy who employs you.”

⁂

Their predictions turned out to be true. Carey House didn’t need another cook, not even a dishwasher. Mark Hopkins had all the help he needed. Including a boy to box up purchases, and even deliver them—for a fee. Abe and Rudolph Seligman didn’t have any work for him, either as a salesperson or stock clerk in their clothing store. J. M. Studebaker had all the help he needed in his blacksmith shop, where he also made wheelbarrows.

No one was looking for a new employee. All seemed wary of a miner who might quit when the weather improved, or the itch to dig for gold grew too strong to resist.

Edward took the article he'd written to the post office.

"Well, hello, E.B." the postmaster greeted him. "Mailing another article to that newspaper of yours?"

Edward smiled. "Yup."

He looked at the name sign, *Thomas C. Nugent, Postmaster*, and had a sudden idea.

"You wouldn't by any chance be looking to hire an assistant, would you?"

Nugent looked thoughtful. "Well… I know you can write." He gave Edward a quizzical look. "Probably even read."

"I went to Indiana Asbury University for two years."

"I'd guess you quit when you got gold fever."

Edward blushed at the truth of Nugent's statement.

"You'd probably quit working here, as soon as your two *compadres* struck it rich again."

"No I wouldn't. I swear!"

"Well… tell you what," Nugent looked serious, "I've a mind to hire you to clerk. Clean up. Deliver to mining camps around.

"Pay wouldn't be what you'd earn on a really good day of mining, but it would be steady. And all yours."

"I could do that!" Edward felt a wave of elation.

"Here's the deal. You work five days a week. Get Tuesdays and Thursdays off. Work Saturdays and Sundays, as well as Monday, Wednesday, Friday.

"And you *will not quit on me…*"

⁂

When he told Richard and Lewis, Edward was disappointed at their reaction.

"Don't think you can get a cut of gold you didn't help mine," Lewis admonished.

"Of course not. I figured we'd split food costs and other joint expenses three ways out of our own money. When you two work without me, you'd split the gold in half, and on my days off, I'd work with you and get my third of the gold."

"I feel sorry for Nugent when you quit because we strike it rich again," commented Richard.

"He doesn't have anything to worry about." Edward laughed. "He said if I quit, he'd stop giving me my mail. I'd have to go all the way to Sacramento to pick it up!"

Chapter Thirty-Four

Friday, Saturday, and Sunday went by in a rush. Nugent had just finished showing Edward how the post office operated, when the stage from Sacramento arrived. Along with passengers, it carried a mailbag for Placerville.

"Put letters for anyone in a business establishment into their Post Office boxes along this wall," Nugent directed. "Mail for individual miners is alphabetized in these larger boxes. Only the person to whom it's addressed can pick up personal mail. If the mail has to be forwarded to one of the mining camps around—Diamond Springs, El Dorado, Coloma, and such—put it into their mail bags, back here."

While Edward was doing that, a group of miners came in to pick up and mail letters.

"Any mail for Perkins?"

"For Geiger?"

"Clark?"

"How much to mail this to St. Louis?" asked one miner, handing Edward a letter.

Edward looked it up in his book. "Forty cents."

The miner measured out gold powder onto a scale. Edward poured the gold into the post office's container, stamped the letter, and placed it in the *Out-Going East* box.

"Any mail for Frink?"

"No," Edward answered, searching through the E through G box of alphabetized letters.

"How about Davis?" the miner asked.

"Which Davis?"

"Jerry."

"Yes, there's one here but I can't give it to you. Davis has to come in and pick it up for himself."

"But, he's my partner. Back up the mountain. He said I should pick it up for him."

"Sorry." Edward empathized, knowing how hard it was for men with isolated claims to get to town. "But this is United States Government mail, and that's the law. Individuals have to come claim their mail *in person."*

With a frown, Frink stomped out the door.

On Saturday, stages arrived from San Francisco, Monterey, and San Jose. Mailbags required sorting, and the lines at the counter grew longer as impatient men came from their claims to spend the weekend in town, shopping and gambling.

By the time Sunday night arrived, Edward's head ached and his eyes felt crossed from trying to decipher illegible handwriting, and even worse spelling.

One more day at the post office, and he'd get a day off! He knew it would get easier as he got used to the routine.

But, for now, he was ready to pass out as soon as his head hit the mattress.

* * *

Bam! Bam!

The loud banging on the door woke all three of them.

"E. B., or whatever the devil your name is, open the door!"

Bam! Bam!

Edward groaned and shivered as his bare feet hit the icy floor.

"Hold your horses!" he shouted. *What's he hitting the door with? Sounds like a pick ax handle.*

A stranger stood at the door, looking disgruntled.

"Who in blazes are you?"

"Jerry Davis! I want my *damned* mail!"

Edward tried to focus his bleary eyes. "Do you have any idea what time it is?"

"Yeah. The middle of the night, and I want my mail. Now!"

"The post office is closed. Come back tomorrow."

"Not going to be here tomorrow. Want my mail now." A crafty look crossed his face. "I've got gold. Make it worth your while—since it's the middle of the night and all."

"Well, I'm awake now. Might as well go down to the post office and get your letter. Just let me get my boots and jacket."

A few minutes later, Edward took the keys out of his pocket and unlocked the front door. *So, this is why Nugent made sure I had keys. So* I *could be dragged out in the middle of the night, instead of him.*

“Here’s your letter,” he said, handing Davis the precious envelope.

“And here’s the gold to pay for the inconvenience.” He weighed out forty dollar’s worth of gold on the scale.

“Thanks! I appreciate that,” Edward answered, now fully awake.

* * *

During lulls in customers, E.B. learned more about the postmaster who had become his boss. Thomas Carr Nugent, at 38, was just six years older than he, but seemed many years more matured.

“Guess fighting in the Mexican-American War made me grow up in a hurry,” Nugent said.

“You were a soldier?” Edward asked, impressed.

“Yep. Enlisted in the Mounted Riflemen. Served under General Winfield Scott during the army’s march from Vera Cruz to Mexico City. Got wounded there. Nothing much.” He held out a hand with a scar still visible.

A miner came in and Edward gave him his mail.

“After the war they offered me a commission in the Regular Army,” Nugent continued, as the miner left, “I said, ‘Thanks, but no thanks.’ Heard about gold in California and decided to try my hand at mining. Went by ship to Panama, hiked across the Isthmus, and sailed up to San Francisco. And, here I am, in what was at that time called Dry Diggin’s.”

"So, why did you give up mining and become the postmaster?" By now Edward could sort mail and carry on a conversation at the same time, without thinking twice.

"Probably the same as you. Mining was hard, grubby work, and the returns unpredictable. I did better when I became manager of the Big Ditch & Gravel Mining Company. We dug a ditch, which tapped into the American River and brought water down for mining. And for the town, too, of course."

"But, that still doesn't tell me why, or how, you became the postmaster."

"On April ninth of this year, the Post Office was first established, and the town selected me as postmaster." Nugent paused in sorting letters and smiled.

"One of the first letters I received from Washington D.C. asked if I could select a different name for the town. I guess they didn't like 'Hangtown.' I suggested 'Placerville,' and everyone in town's been arguing the matter ever since."

❊ ❊ ❊

The following Monday afternoon, as Nugent turned the sign in the front window from OPEN to CLOSED he said, "Soon as you get the floor cleaned up, you can go home. Day off tomorrow."

Edward looked down with disgust. A week's worth of mud, spit and tobacco covered the floor, obliterating any sign of the wood beneath.

"I suggest you use a shovel to start," Nugent continued. "Then a broom and dust pan." He paused. "Might want to dump it all into that canvas bag in the box in the corner."

He turned to leave.

"Why?" Edward asked.

"Why, what?"

"Why dump all that trash in the bag. Why not just shovel it out in the street?"

"You might want to take it home."

Edward frowned. "Take it *home?"*

"Might want to run it through a gold pan."

"A *gold* pan?"

"Men get clumsy when they pour out gold to pay for postage. Sometimes spill a little on the floor in their hurry. You sweep it—you keep it."

Nugent smiled over his shoulder as he went out the door. "Might mine more gold in the trash than your friends do on a middling day at the Long Tom!"

Chapter Thirty-Five

"Morning, boss," Edward said as he entered the post office on Wednesday morning.

"Morning, E.B." Nugent looked up from the letters he was sorting. "Don't take off your jacket. I need you to take the mail to Coloma this morning."

"Coloma? Isn't that where gold was first discovered?"

"The very same."

"I remember reading about it in a St. Louis newspaper in '48. I wrote an article about it for *The Argus.*

"Just a couple of years," he continued, "and it seems like that day—reading the article—happened an eon ago, to someone else. Not me."

"Yep," Nugent agreed, nodding his head. "Leave Greencastle, Indiana, and travel all the way across the country to California. Different state. Different life. Makes you feel like a different man."

"Where *is* Coloma, and how do I get there?"

"You haven't been there before?"

"I haven't been *anywhere* in California, except Sacramento for the statehood celebration."

"You'll get a horse from the livery, here in town. The post office has an account. They'll fix you up with a good enough animal to get you to Coloma and back. Turn right just outside of town and follow the wagon tracks straight north till you get there. About nine, ten miles, I'd reckon."

* * *

Riding the chestnut filly through Placerville, Edward felt like a schoolboy skipping classes. The town was quiet, all the miners busy on their claims in the hills. It was still too early for mule or ox-drawn wagons to arrive from Sacramento. They'd soon be taking their strangely assorted cargoes to the various stores and other business establishments.

Edward took a deep breath, and felt like singing. The air, after the rain, was crisp and fresh. The hills had turned yellow and red with fall foliage. The peaks of the High Sierras, mantled in snow from the recent storms, glistened white against a cobalt sky.

No one around. No sounds but the twittering of birds, the soft clip-clop of hooves treading on fallen leaves, and the rustle of a gentle breeze in the trees. When was the last time he had traveled anywhere without being part of a group? He felt jubilantly, gloriously free.

The sight of Coloma, somewhat over an hour later, came as a surprise. There must have been two or three hundred frame homes and several large hotels. Not shanties, log cabins, and tents like Placerville. Of course, Edward realized, there's a sawmill here. Gold was *discovered* at the sawmill!

Edward dropped off the mailbag at the post office.

"You can feed and water your horse at the stable, just down the street," the Coloma postmaster said. "And if you're interested in dinner, the best food in town is at Nancy Gooch's. She and Peter arrived earlier this year. They were slaves, but their owners freed them when they got to California. Ask anyone in town. They can direct you."

After taking care of his horse, Edward walked around a bit. The town bustled with miners down from the hills, shopkeepers, and townsfolk. But, the mill dominated the scene with a cacophony of whining, screeching saws, and shouting men.

Edward stared at the long, narrow, open platform on raised footings. It stood in the shade of an overhead roof. This was the true center of Coloma, the bulwark of its economy.

Passing Bekeart's Store and a bakery, he made his way at last, to Nancy's. Opening the door, he felt suddenly overcome by homesickness.

"This smells like my mother's kitchen," he told Nancy as she smiled a welcome from the kitchen, behind the pass-through to the dining room. He sniffed again. "Baked ham, molasses, fresh-baked corn bread, and, can it be, sweet potato pie?"

"Yes, sir. You done smelled real good. Sit anywhere. I'm just servin' up."

Edward saw two trestle tables, set up for twelve people each. Five men were already seated at empty place settings, watching expectantly as Nancy began putting platters on the pass-through.

The closest man waved off her admonition to stay put, and brought the platters to the table. Beside the ham and corn bread, there came mashed potatoes swimming in melted butter, fresh greens, and pickled beets. The sweet potato pies arrived last.

"Name's Fred," said a man as he passed the ham.

"Edward," he responded. "From the post office in Placerville."

"You brought mail?" asked a man sitting across the table from him.

"Yes, I did." Edward took a bite of ham. "This is real southern cooking."

"You from the south?"

"Virginia," Edward answered. "At least I was born there. My folks go back all the way to colonial times. We moved to Indiana when I was eight. But my mother still cooks meals just like this."

"Hey, everyone," called out the man opposite, "the mail's in. Edward, here, just brought it!"

Nancy beamed from the kitchen. "Dinner's on the house for the U.S. Postal Service," she declared.

"No, ma'am," Edward said, swallowing. "I'll pay, willingly, for such a fine meal."

From the talk around the table, he learned Coloma had a population of ten thousand. And although miners were already beginning to leave for places like Placerville and others, the town was secure as the county seat. By the time Edward finished, every chair, bench and stool was taken, and more men stood waiting, hats in hand.

He already realized, Wednesdays—delivering the mail to Coloma, with lunch at Nancy's—would become the highlight of his week.

Edward knew better than to try convincing either Richard or Lewis, but life in California was about more than gold.

Much more.

Chapter Thirty-Six

Low gray clouds obliterated any view of mountains, as they wept cold rain. Even with coal oil lamps burning, the post office seemed dark and gloomy.

Edward and Nugent sorted through bags of mail on this Monday morning in late February, putting local miners' letters in their alphabetized slots, mail for other mining camps in their postal bags, and Placerville business mail into their boxes.

"Hey, E. B." Nugent called out. "Here's a letter for you! Looks to be from your folks in Greencastle."

Suddenly the room seemed brighter. "My first letter from home! I wondered how long it would take. Let me see it."

November 18, 1850
Dear Son,

We were overjoyed to receive your letter from California. My, what a relief to know all three of you arrived safe and sound! We look forward to more letters detailing your trip to California and your life there.

By now, you must know California is a state in the Union. Just knowing California is part of America makes you seem closer...

"I wrote to them when we first arrived last August," Edward commented. "If I remember correctly, we'd just gotten our cabin and started mining. We didn't know a soul here, or what we were doing."

Edward shook his head, with a slight smile. "And now I'm working in the post office, and know almost every miner on the mountain. And the owners of all the stores and establishments in town are friends.

"When they wrote this letter, they didn't know any of that. The time lag between letters makes it seem as though they're on the other side of the moon, not just across the continent from here."

Just then, several men came in, shaking water from their hats, and scraping mud from their boots. During the flurry of activity—weighing out gold powder, putting stamps on envelopes, searching for letters among the in-coming mail, Edward stuck his own letter in his pocket.

It'll keep, he thought, and Richard and Lewis will want to hear it, too.

❊ ❊ ❊

"How come you got a letter and we didn't?" asked Lewis.

"Probably because I wrote one to my family, and you didn't," Edward retorted. "You'll get letters. I know my folks will share the news with both of yours. They'll write soon. It just takes forever to get mail from Greencastle to here."

Edward read the whole letter to Richard and Lewis, ending with...

We're all fine, and hope you're in good health. Eliza is thinking of taking up where you left off, and enrolling in Indiana Asbury University. She says she wants to be a schoolteacher when she grows up. Lawrence is jealous of your grand luck in going to California. He keeps saying, by the time he gets old enough, there won't be any adventures left for him. Susanna says to tell you 'hello' from her.

With all our love,

Mother

Silence descended as Edward finished reading the letter. The fire popped in the stove. A mood of nostalgia pervaded the cabin.

Susanna, Edward thought, *I wonder if she'll still be waiting for me when I get home?*

He tried, without success, to picture her in Placerville. He couldn't even imagine her surviving the rigors of traveling across the country in a covered wagon, let alone adapting to life in this rambunctious town.

Would he want to marry her when he returned to Greencastle? He pictured himself, finishing the university, working for *The Argus*, writing up the events of the church ladies' guild. Why did he feel so depressed? Was it just homesickness?

Chapter Thirty-Seven

As usual, come dinnertime on a Wednesday, Edward was seated at a long table at Nancy's in Coloma.

"Hey, E.B.," said Thomas Springer, sitting across from him, "have you seen our newspaper?"

"You've got a newspaper here? In Coloma?"

"Yup! First paper published in the Mother Lode." Springer's chest puffed with pride. "In fact, it's the first paper outside of Sacramento, in the interior of the state."

"Your very own newspaper," Edward commented. "What will they think of next? Coloma's getting very civilized."

Springer handed a copy of the paper across the table. "My partner's F.A. Harmon. He's with the *Sacramento Union*, as well. Knows what he's doing."

"The El Dorado News, Saturday, July 12, 1851," Edward read.

"I'd like to buy a copy. Take it home to read." He paused. Smiled. "You know, I worked for the town newspaper back in Indiana. Still send them articles from time to time. This," he waved the paper, "brings back a lot of memories."

Edward took his copy home with him so he could share it with Richard and Lewis. There wasn't much church news, he noted. Like Placerville, there were churches in Coloma, but they were lucky to have services on Sundays. Even the ministers were more interested in mining gold than counseling parishioners.

Berkeart's Store had an ad in the paper, he noted, as did Luther Davis, for his bakery and confectionery store, and William Hooper, for his fresh-grown fruits and vegetables.

"Here's an interesting article," Edward announced. "It's a letter from a Doctor LaFayette Houghton Bunnell, of the Mariposa Battalion. It seems they were chasing some Indians south of here, down by the San Joaquin and Merced rivers.

"They'd come upon an amazing valley guarded by gigantic solid granite cliffs.

"He says here... *To obtain a more distinct and quiet view, I had left the trail and my horse and I wallowed through the snow alone to a projecting granite rock...*

"Hmmm," Edward continued reading, "it seems his Major called him from the rear of the column and said, *You had better wake up from that dream up there, or you may lose your hair; I have no faith in Ten-ie-ya's statement there are no Indians about here. We had better be moving; some of the murdering devils may be lurking along this trail to pick off stragglers.* To which Bunnell responded, *If my hair is now required, I can depart in peace, for I have seen the power and glory of a Supreme Being; the majesty of His handy-work is in the Testimony of the Rocks."*

Edward continued reading, while Richard and Lewis waited for the end of the article.

"That night," Edward reported, "the men sat around the campfire, trying to decide what to call this remarkable valley. Finally they decided it should be an American name, not something from Europe, or in Latin.

In the end, this Bunnell suggested giving it the name of the Indian tribe they were displacing—calling the valley *Yo-sem-i-ty. By so doing,* he says, *the name of the tribe of Indians which we met leaving their homes in the valley, perhaps never to return, would be perpetuated."*

A silence followed Edward's reading of the newspaper article.

"Too bad we're leaving in a couple of weeks," Richard said. "We'll never have a chance to see this *Yo-sem-i-ty* Valley."

Chapter Thirty-Eight

As time approached to leave California for home, the intensity level in their cabin rose. Richard and Lewis cursed the fact that the long summer days were shortening by seconds as July drew to a close. As long as there was enough light to see, they were at their claim, mining gold—or chasing dead-ends.

"I need all the gold I can get," Lewis declared, "to buy a farm and build a house. Then Elizabeth and I can get married, without having to live with my family. We'll be independent!"

"I don't know *exactly* what I'll do." Richard's voice changed. "Even though I *hate* mining!" He glared at Lewis, "I damned well want to take all the gold we can get before we leave."

Lewis grinned. "I hate it too, but I'm not going to quit until the day we pack up the wagon and head for Greencastle."

"Just think," Richard said with a smile, "sleeping in a bed with fresh sheets, living in a clean house, delicious meals on the table three times a day—every single day, church on Sunday, good times with friends on Saturday night…"

Edward looked back and forth between the two of them. Although having agreed to leave, he couldn't get all that worked up over scrabbling for gold and more gold to take with him before they left.

They had met other miners who were planning on leaving Placerville toward the end of August.

"We can make it one year to the day, if we leave on August 20th," Edward commented, wondering why the idea didn't thrill him.

"August twentieth, September twentieth, October twentieth…" Richard counted off on his fingers; "we might make it to Indiana before snowfall."

"It'll depend on the others. We're better off traveling in a group," Lewis reminded him.

In the end, the group of four wagons decided to compromise, and leave on August fifteenth.

* * *

As Nugent was turning the sign to CLOSED on Wednesday, August sixth, Edward said, "Boss, I… I've got something… something to tell you."

Nugent looked at him, one eyebrow raised.

"I… we… Richard, Lewis, and I are going home, to Greencastle, on the fifteenth."

"You're what?"

"We're going home. We only planned to stay a year. Have an adventure. Get some gold. See the country," Edward explained in a rush. "But now, the year's up and they're anxious to go back…" he swallowed, "home."

"And you?" Nugent asked. "What do *you* want?"

Edward looked at the scuffed toes of his boots. "I actually *like* it here, but I promised to go back. They're planning on me going with them. And my family expects me to, as well."

"Well, I hate to see you go." Nugent's glare softened. "You can always let me know if you change your mind."

"Yes, sir. But I… don't think I'll be doing that."

✻ ✻ ✻

"I hate to spend time out from mining, to buy a wagon and oxen," Lewis complained that night.

"Let E.B. do it," Richard said. "He's not breaking his back mining. He can go to Sacramento tomorrow on his day off and bring back oxen and a wagon."

Richard gave Edward his best smile. "You will, won't you?"

Edward felt a tinge of apprehension. "It's a huge responsibility. What if I can't find a wagon and oxen we think will survive the trip?"

✻ ✻ ✻

The next day, Edward had dinner at the boarding house with Caroline, which he did occasionally on his day off.

"Land's sakes, E.B.!" she declared. "I never thought you'd go back, after all the trouble we went to, to get here."

"We never intended to stay." His throat tightened up at the thought of leaving Caroline and Ellen. Right now, they seemed more like family than his own in faraway Greencastle.

"Well, I'll miss you, boy. And Ellen will too, I know."

Edward smiled. "I can't believe she's eleven. I haven't seen her since the statehood celebration last October."

"She's doing real well in boarding school. I see her often, of course. Growing like a weed. She asks about you. Seems glad we keep in touch."

"Tell her I'll miss her when we leave. But I'll write to you both when we get home."

"You be sure and do that." She closed her eyes and shook her head. "But, it won't be the same."

Caroline hugged him hard when he left after dinner. Edward's throat grew tight again, and his eyes filled with unshed tears.

He needed to find a wife, he decided, resolutely. He couldn't think of anyone he'd met since arriving in California that he'd actually wed. He loved Caroline, of course, but she was so much older, more like a favorite aunt, than wife.

And, Susanna was evidently still available in Greencastle.

* * *

The sun was setting, making the golden hills glow in soft after-light, when Edward came rolling into Placerville. Seated on the bench of a covered wagon, he drove four head of oxen, his horse tied on behind. He knew he was grinning from ear to ear.

Men stopped and shouted at him as the wagon rolled past.

"Hey E.B., where you goin' in that rig?"

"You're not leaving Placerville, are you?"

"Are you moving?"

"Sacramento?"

"San Francisco?"

"We're going home. Back to Indiana. All three of us!" he called out, suddenly eager to get under way.

They spent the next week packing up by lamplight, Richard and Lewis still unwilling to spend any daylight hours away from mining. They took all their clothes, of course, and cooking utensils. They agreed to take only enough food to get over the Sierras.

"Keep the wagon as light as we can," Richard reiterated. "We can get provisions in Rag Town."

Edward remembered the fresh vegetables growing in every kitchen garden—and the abundant, clear water of Carson River.

"We'll get barrels for water there," he said, shuddering as he thought about Humboldt Sink and the desert beyond.

* * *

In the pitch-black of the night before they were to meet up with the other wagons at daybreak, Edward suddenly sat up in bed. His heart pounded. He could hardly catch his breath.

What awakened me, he questioned? Was it a sound? I can't hear anything. Not even crickets chirping or frogs burping. Why am I awake, my heart thumping, like a wild thing against my ribs?

Edward crawled out of bed. Put on his pants and boots. He stumbled out the door, and by moonlight pawed through the packed wagon.

"What in the *hell* are you doing?" Richard's voice was thick with sleep.

"Taking out my clothes."

"You're *what?"*

"Taking my clothes. I'm not going back. I'm staying here in California!"

* * *

As he waved goodbye to the four wagons the next morning—Richard and Lewis shaking their heads in bewilderment—Edward had but one thought.

Am I making the biggest mistake of my life?

Chapter Thirty-Nine

Friday, August 15, 1851

Dear Family,

I don't know which will arrive in Greencastle first, this letter or Richard and Lewis. I sort of hope the letter does, because Richard and Lewis won't be able to explain why I'm not on the covered wagon with them. I'm not sure I can explain it, either, but I'll try.

First of all, don't worry. I'm perfectly fine. Maybe a little crazy, but in good health and spirits.

We were all packed up and ready to go, when I suddenly felt this was wrong for me. I haven't experienced enough of California. At first, I was like most of the men here, wanting the adventure of traveling across the vast expanse of this amazing land. And, eager to dig up lots of gold.

That's what Richard and Lewis wanted, and that's what they did. They were more than ready to stop mining and get back to Greencastle and the life they had there.

But, I started working in the post office and met more men here who have done other kinds of jobs. I wouldn't have stayed to keep digging more gold. However, I foresee lots of possibilities here—besides gold.

I've made a list of pros and cons of staying on in California for the near future.

On the pro side, I'm excited! California is growing. There are all kinds of opportunities here. And more cropping up every day.

I get a real kick out of the energy of the mining camps and towns I've seen. I want to experience more towns before I say 'good-bye' to California forever. I want to meet more people. Try more jobs.

Placerville is growing by leaps and bounds. Several families live here now. The Methodist Church is beginning to take a more active part in people's lives.

On the con side, I miss my family. And I know, at age 23, I should be settling down. Pursuing a career. Getting married and starting a family.

But, do you remember how you felt when you left Virginia to go to Indiana? Well, I want to be a part of what California becomes as it moves forward as a state.

I hope you're not too disappointed in me. I'll continue to write and let you know what I'm doing. And, more than likely, I'll show up at your door one day, satisfied I've seen and done all that California has to offer, and more than ready to settle down in Greencastle.

Please know, I love you all.

Your son,

E.B.

* * *

Edward took the letter to the post office, where Nugent didn't seem all that surprised to see him.

"Is it too late to get my old job back?"

"I told you I'd save it for you. Besides, there's a possibility of a different job you might like to try."

"Oh? What's that?"

"Have you ever driven a stagecoach?"

The idea sent Edward's head spinning. *To crack a whip over a team of horses as the stage careened down the road, sending a cloud of dust billowing behind!* That's *why I wasn't ready to go back to Indiana!*

"Do you think I could?"

"Don't see why not," the postmaster said. "Others have done it. And you're no worse than them."

"But... what about working for the post office?"

"We could arrange a schedule. Besides, you'd be carrying mail as well as passengers and packages."

"When would I start? Learning, I mean."

"Shouldn't be too long. We'll find someone to teach you. Work as an apprentice till you learn the ropes. I know Barton & Ellison are always looking to hire experienced teamsters."

* * *

Edward arranged to rent rooms in the cabin to two miners who were thrilled to move in from their tent. They took the two empty bedrooms, and he had already moved his clothes back into the one he had been using.

All of Edward's cooking utensils had gone back to Indiana on the covered wagon, but the new miners had sufficient equipment for the simple cooking they needed.

Edward slipped into a comfortable routine—working five days a week, with Tuesdays and Thursdays off. On those off days, he was learning to handle horses bred to work in teams, pulling coaches at a fast clip. These horses were nothing like farm animals, pulling a plow. And, he shook his head in amazement, how different they were from the placid oxen that had pulled their covered wagon across the continent!

Edward loved the breath-taking exhilaration. The speed. The feel of wind blowing past his face. But he never lost sight of the responsibility that would be his—of being in charge of the team, stage, and passengers—when one day he was hired to drive all by himself.

Meanwhile, he threw himself into learning to be the best darn stagecoach driver in all of California!

❊ ❊ ❊

Months after the events, letters arrived from Greencastle.

Sunday, October 26, 1851

Dear Son,

It is my sad duty to inform you, your cousin, little George, Uncle John and Aunt Sarah's son, has died. He was only two years, eight months and one day old. He is to be buried in Forest Hill Cemetery, here in Greencastle. We are all devastated...

He was just a baby, Edward thought. Born about the time word of California's gold discovery was beginning to spread. A babe in arms at family Sunday dinners.

And then, two months later, came even more staggering news.

Thursday, December 18, 1851

Dear Son,

How sad it is, to write to you so soon, with more heartbreaking news. Your cousin, John Chenoweth, with whom you played as a boy, has followed his little brother George, in death. He was just over 19 when he died. I don't know how my brother and Sarah can bear the pain...

John! Dead! Halfway in age between Eliza and me, Edward thought. The words on the page didn't seem real to him. Poor Uncle John and Aunt Sarah.

His two cousins had died and been buried in 1851, and he didn't even know about it until well into 1852. The distance between him and his family seemed even greater than ever.

* * *

The next two letters were of a more cheerful nature. On February eighteenth, the first railroad arrived in Greencastle. And about the same time, an Albert Patrick had started a competing newspaper, the *Putnam Republican Banner.*

But all the news from home, both good and bad, made Edward feel even more cut off, more removed from his family and the town in which he'd grown up. Had he been wrong to remain in California? Was it too late to go back now? Would he want to?

Well, not just yet. He was almost ready to become a teamster and drive a stagecoach on his own. He couldn't quit California until he'd at least put this new skill to the test!

Chapter Forty

It took a lot longer to qualify as a teamster than Edward had realized. It wasn't enough to know how to take care of the spirited horses, and make emergency repairs on the tack or coach. Learning to handle one, two, or three pairs of reins, separating the lead team from the wheel horses, and occasionally middle ones as well—without getting his own fingers tangled up in the leather—was a hard-won skill.

Then he had to learn the various routes. Edward had nightmares about getting lost—the stagecoach filled with passengers, and he couldn't figure out which faint set of wheel tracks in the dust to follow. Or he'd be traveling at break-neck speed, on and on, only to realize he'd passed the same landmark three times!

He also needed to memorize where to stop in each camp or town—which would be rest stops, which meal stops, and at what hotel or diner. He had to know where to drop off and pick up mail, packages, and passengers.

All this, while still working at least four days a week at the post office.

But at last, the day of certification arrived. Edward knew someone from Barton & Ellison would ride with him, evaluating his performance as a stagecoach driver. He couldn't remember when he had been more nervous.

He loaded canvas mailbags into the boot of the stagecoach, each labeled with its destination: Plymouth, Drytown, Jackson, Mokelumne Hill. Although the early spring day was cool, Edward's palms were sweaty inside his leather gloves.

He jerked the reins and called out, "Get up."

To his vast relief, the horses—two matched pairs—pulled the shiny wooden coach with bright yellow trim down the street to the hotel. Here, a traveling salesman made ready to board. Two large suitcases stood on the wooden sidewalk. Ignoring them, the salesman doffed his fedora to Edward and climbed to his seat inside the coach, without so much as a speck of dust on his woolen suit and white boiled shirt.

With a grunt, Edward heaved the smaller suitcase to the rack on top. He tried to lift the larger case. It didn't even budge. *What is he selling?* Edward wondered. *Anvils?*

A couple of men walked by just then, and helped hoist it next to the suitcase.

"Thank you!" Edward said, shaking their hands. "You don't by any chance want to ride the coach to Jackson, so you can help me get that bugger down, do you?"

"No thanks, friend," they chorused.

Just then, a woman with two small children emerged. Hotel workers brought a steamer trunk and a smaller valise. The woman kept a firm grip on the boy, whom Edward judged to be about three years old, and the baby girl, perhaps a little over one year.

The woman smiled at Edward. "We're going all the way to Mokelumne Hill."

"Yes, ma'am." He noticed she was quite thin, pale, with dark smudges under her eyes. "Are you all right, ma'am?"

She sighed. Looked at each of her children. "I will be, as soon as I get to Mokelumne."

As they settled into the coach, the hotel workers helped Edward get the steamer trunk on the rack, along with the valise.

"Is that everyone?" Edward called. "Stagecoach leaving for El Dorado, Plymouth, Drytown, Sutter Creek, Jackson, and Mokelumne Hill!"

Edward sprang to the driver's seat, trying not to notice The Man, sitting next to him. The Man said nothing, as he noted the time on his pocket watch, and wrote something in a notebook. He then stared straight ahead, without any expression.

"Get up!" Edward called to the horses, flicking the four sets of reins he held in his hand. The stagecoach started rolling majestically down the narrow main street. Edward sat straight, feeling confident in his new leather pants and jacket, wide-brimmed hat pulled firmly down on his forehead. He was in control of this coach. Of the spirited black horses pulling it. Of the passengers and baggage.

If only I could figure out what The Man is thinking, Edward fretted.

As soon as they left Placerville, Edward cracked the whip. Although the road was somewhat steep and winding, the dirt was hard-packed. This was where he hoped he could make time on the trip. "Come on, team!" he encouraged, flicking the whip well above their heads.

"El Dorado!" Edward shouted some fifteen minutes later, as he pulled hard on the reins. "Five minute stop! Outhouse behind the post office! Next stop Plymouth!"

He hopped down and put a box labeled Jackson, waiting in front of the post office, on top of the coach.

Within ten minutes, they were on their way again.

The road went through some fairly level areas, beautifully green in new spring leaves and grasses. Here he urged the horses on to greater speed. But he remembered a stage that had been going too fast, very near here. The rear wheel hit a boulder, just as the front wheel went into a small ditch.

The stage tipped over, killing the driver and another man sitting next to him. Three passengers inside had serious injuries. The axel broke. Several hours passed before anyone came to help the injured. And it took until the next day before the coach could be repaired and the journey continued.

His heart pounding in his chest, Edward pulled lightly on the reins, watching ahead for rocks and boulders. Was he going too slowly? He urged the horses on, just a bit faster. If only he knew what the silent man next to him was thinking.

Every once in a while, as the road went up or down a hill, a grade slowed their progress. Downhill was, if anything, even more dangerous than up. He practically stood on the brake pedal, to keep the coach from pushing the horses from behind.

Edward couldn't help but keep glancing at The Man. His blank expression gave nothing away. Other than checking his pocket watch and jotting notes in the book, he stared straight ahead. No expression. No word.

"Plymouth!" Edward shouted. "Forty-five minute lunch stop. Out house behind the hotel restaurant."

He helped the passengers down the coach steps, took the Plymouth mailbag to the post office, and picked up their bags for Jackson, and Mokelumne Hill. He led the horses to the livery stable where hands would feed, water, curry, and check for pebbles in their hooves—or any other possible injuries.

After taking advantage of the outhouse, Edward washed his hands and face in the basin on a counter just outside the back door to the dining room.

Inside, The Man sat by himself at a table in a back corner. The salesman had picked up a newspaper and was reading it as he ate at another table.

"Would you care to join us?" invited the mother, indicating an empty chair.

"Oh, yes!" exclaimed the little boy, bouncing on his chair and looking with hero-worship at Edward.

Edward smiled. He knew he would have been just as impressed at that age, with any adult who could make the horses run and the stagecoach go so fast.

"Thank you, I would."

As they ate, he learned the lady's name was Abigail, her children Charity and William. They were on their way to meet husband-and-father, who'd staked a claim near Mok Hill, as he referred to it in his letters. He'd sent money for the three of them to join him from Boston. They'd already sailed down the East Coast to Panama, and then crossed the Isthmus, to pick up another boat to San Francisco and Sacramento.

"While we were on the Isthmus, I became ill. I got separated from the Indians who carried our belongings, and my son. I had Charity and the valise with me, but William and our steamer trunk went on with another group. Of course, we couldn't understand a word the Indians said, and the man who had organized us didn't know where they had gone, either.

"I was more sick with fear than from dysentery, positive I'd never see my son again."

What could possibly be worse for a mother? "But, you did get together again." Edward smiled, looking at William's shining eyes.

"Yes. When we got to the Pacific Ocean a sailing ship was waiting for us, and, magically, there was my son… and our steamer trunk! Along with several other small groups the Indians had led."

Abigail smiled and ruffled her fingers through the boy's hair. "I'm not going to let him out of my sight again until he's at least thirty years old!"

❊ ❊ ❊

Leaving Plymouth—Drytown, Amador City, Sutter Creek, and Jackson came in quick succession. Mailbags were exchanged; parcels and boxes delivered and picked up. A miner with a knapsack boarded in Drytown and got off in Jackson. He and the postmaster in Jackson helped Edward wrestle down the salesman's heavy trunk. The owner then requisitioned help from the hotel to get it delivered there.

After a twenty-minute rest stop in Jackson, they finally arrived at Mok Hill in late afternoon.

Abigail's husband met the family as the stagecoach came to a stop.

"Daddy!" shouted William, jumping down the steps and scampering to his father's open arms. Soon Abigail and Charity were enveloped, along with William, in a giant four-way bear hug.

Edward smiled, knowing what the family had gone through to arrive here. What stories they would have!

He watched as the father pushed his wheelbarrow down the street. William waved from his perch on top of the steamer trunk while Abigail followed carrying Charity.

Edward looked around for The Man, but he had disappeared. Scanning the street, he saw only strangers. Each going his own way. Ignoring him completely.

But, Edward thought, *this was to be my certification day. A sort of final exam after all my hard work. And I was sure The Man was the one who was going to evaluate my performance. Did I keep on schedule? Drive too slow, or too fast? Did I stop at all the right stops? Remember to get my log signed at every one?*

Edward shoved his hat back and scratched his head.

How do I find out whether I passed or not?

Chapter Forty-One

What do I do now?

He took the stagecoach to the livery, unhitched the horses, and helped the stableman water, brush, and curry them. With the horses in stalls, contentedly munching hay, and the coach washed and parked behind the livery, Edward slung his saddlebag over his shoulder and walked to the hotel where a room was reserved for the stagecoach driver.

As he was signing the hotel register, Edward felt a tap on his shoulder.

The Man. As they shook hands, he said, "Good job. You're hired to take the weekly route from Placerville to Mok Hill on Mondays, returning on Tuesdays."

With that, he turned and went into the dining room.

Edward felt like shouting with joy, but kept his response to a whispered "Yes!"

A few months later, on a special 1852 census, he proudly entered his occupation as "teamster."

❊ ❊ ❊

Meanwhile, he was feeling more and more disgusted with his living accommodations. The cabin hadn't been so bad with Richard and Lewis as mates. They'd been busy mining, and he'd been content, exploring Placerville and working in the post office.

But now he stayed away as much as he could from the dark, dirt-floored, cramped log cabin. He rarely saw the two miners who slept in the other bedrooms. They cooked for themselves—as evidenced by dirty pots and pans left soaking in a tub of cold, scummy water.

Richard and Lewis had taken their cooking utensils with them, and Edward felt disinclined to replace them to cook for himself. He ate most of his dinners at the growing number of restaurants in Placerville. He supplemented his meals with fresh fruits from the general store, and goods from the bakery.

Nugent and John (J.M. for John Mohler) Studebaker usually joined in his meals. J.M. had moved his wheelbarrow business from Coloma to Placerville, selling them for $10 each. As they got better acquainted, Edward learned John had left his father and five brothers in South Bend, Indiana, with fifty cents in his pocket, trading his wagon for passage to Hangtown. He first settled in Coloma, where besides making wheelbarrows, he also made pickaxes and repaired stagecoaches. He planned to return to South Bend one day, with enough money to invest in the family carriage business, to make it a more profitable concern.

The butcher, Philip Armour, and even Thomas Springer, who, with Harmon, had moved the *El Dorodo News* to Placerville, formed Edward's social network.

After taking the stagecoach route on Mondays and Tuesdays, Edward still delivered the mail to Coloma on

Wednesdays, took Thursdays and Fridays off, and worked at the post office on the weekends.

Finally, revolted by the cabin, Edward decided he had to move out. But where to live? There weren't any vacant houses, and he didn't want to pay to live in a boarding house or hotel.

The only answer was to build a house for himself.

Does this mean I'm staying here? Never going back to Indiana?

Not necessarily.

When I want to go back, I should be able to sell the house and make a good profit.

Edward bought a lot on Coloma Street in Placerville, just above the Episcopal Church. On several of his Wednesday deliveries to the post office in Coloma, he hauled back lumber from Sutter's sawmill for his new house on a flatbed wagon pulled by oxen.

As soon as he had the materials on site, Edward found several miners who had experience in building, and were willing to work with him—for a fee—on Thursdays and Fridays. Even though they might have made more mining—on a good day—here they were guaranteed to earn something every Thursday and Friday.

Occasionally, the men would work on their own, knowing Edward would pay them. What a treat for him to come home from his two-day stint driving stage to Mok Hill and back, to see progress on his home had been made in his absence. He loved every board and nail that went into building his own home.

❋ ❋ ❋

June 13, 1852

Dear Parents,

It's a lovely sunny day in June, and my new house is finally finished! I wish you could see it. There's a proper front porch with a white railing. I've ordered a swing for it, to be delivered from Sacramento next week. The house is painted a soft blue with white trim and shutters. It's two stories, like most of them in our neighborhood.

It has a parlor, dining room and large kitchen downstairs, and four bedrooms upstairs.

I know, you're asking what does a bachelor need with four bedrooms, but as I told you in my last letter, I'll sell the house when I decide to move back to Greencastle, and I'll get a lot more money if it has four bedrooms.

The rest of my immediate furniture is due on the same shipment as the porch swing. A kitchen table and chairs (the stove's already in) and a proper bed, dresser and clothes press for my bedroom. The rest of the house is empty, but I'll fill it up, little by little.

I'm bringing Caroline up next Friday to see the house and have dinner in the hotel. (She's hiring a lady to cook dinner at her boarding house that day.) Ellen will come too, because even though she lives in the boarding school, she doesn't have regular classes in the summer. She's twelve now, and quite the little lady.

I'm hiring a miner's wife to come on Fridays after I'm settled. She'll clean and cook dinner, leaving a cold supper as well. I've given her permission to put whatever cooking utensils she needs on my account at the mercantile. Now I'll be able to invite friends over for cold supper after I finish up at the post office on Fridays.

Edward decided not to include the information that his friends would probably stay to play a friendly game of poker at his kitchen table after their meal. It was innocent enough entertainment among the locals. Nugent, Studebaker, Springer, Armour, and the others, worked too hard for their money to throw it away on the high-stakes poker played in the saloons. But still, he wasn't sure how his parents would feel about playing cards.

Thank you for your last letter. It's so good to hear from you. Tell Eliza to keep up with her studies. She'll make a fine teacher, unless she gets married to one of her beaus. And tell Lawrence there's still plenty of adventure left for him.

My love to you all,

E.B.

Edward folded and addressed his letter. He walked to the post office to mail it, and then went up the hill to Coloma Street. Standing there in the late afternoon sun, looking at his house, he couldn't help but smile at the beauty of white curlicues against the blue exterior.

Later that night, lying in his log cabin bed, waiting for sleep to come, he mentally walked through every room of his new house. He could hardly wait for the furniture to arrive, so he could move in. It would be easy. He had little else than his clothes to take with him.

He sighed. *All I need now is a wife with whom to share the house.*

He wanted, no, *needed* someone to share his life. To hold close. Love. Come home to at the end of the day. Sit with on the porch swing while they admired the view. To talk and make plans for a future *together.*

Edward truly couldn't imagine Susanna making the horrendous trip across the country. Couldn't picture her being happy in rough and ready Placerville. And, even though she'd been a good friend, he was pretty sure he'd never been in love with her. And for all he knew, she might have found someone else to plan a wedding around by now.

Nor could he picture marrying Rose. He refused to feel guilty for visiting her at the saloon every once in a while. She was willing and he was more than needy. He always arrived spruced up and smelling nice. Treated her gently. She seemed to enjoy their… what they did in bed together. But, he was in no way in love with her. Nor she with him.

Who else was there? Caroline? There had been that one time, crossing the Humboldt—but they had never acknowledged, nor mentioned it again. And, while he did love her, in sort of the way he loved his favorite younger aunt; he couldn't picture Caroline as a *wife.*

Where could he meet marriageable women his age? He sighed again. Not in Placerville. Maybe he should go back to Greencastle. If not for Susanna, there'd be others there.

He rolled over and pulled up the covers.

Not until I live a while in my new house!

Chapter Forty-Two

June 1853

A year after having moved into his new house, Edward sat on the porch swing, reading a letter from his mother. Noticing the date the letter was written, he shook his head. It never ceased to amaze him he was reading about events that had taken place four months before.

February 22, 1853

Dear Son,

Your friend, Lewis, asked that I write to you...

"He would," Edward said to no one there. "He'd never think to write a letter, himself."

He and Elizabeth Priest were married yesterday in Simpson Chapel, which was built shortly after you left for California. Beth looked lovely, and Lewis, proud and handsome. They even managed to get fresh flowers from somewhere for the bride's bouquet.

Simpson Chapel turned out to be a very nice-looking building, being of brick and two stories. It's on the corner of College Avenue and Seminary Street.

Lewis has done well for himself since returning from California. He evidently returned with a sufficiency of gold to buy a farm, construct a commodious house and barn, and refurbish the original dwelling for a hired family...

Edward put the letter down, and rocked gently back and forth. He looked out over the ravine in which Placerville spread out before him. Would he rather have been on his own farm in Indiana?

Well, not a farm. He was no farmer. But, would he rather be sitting in a house like this one, in Greencastle? Unable to answer that question, he returned to the letter in his hand.

I know envy is a sin, but I must admit a twinge of jealousy for Lewis' parents, who have their son home again after his fine adventure. They can look forward to holding grandchildren on their knees.

Nevertheless, you are an adult, and must make your own decisions about your life.

A shaft of guilt speared him. He had always been the "good son," protector of his younger sister, role model for happy-go-lucky Lawrence; his parents' eldest child; their pride and joy.

Then, he'd dropped out of school, much to his mother's dismay, and come to California. Now, he was obviously being selfish, continuing to live in California for another year. But, damn it, he liked his life here! And he loved his home.

Oh well, he thought, it's barely June. I'll think about selling my house and returning to Indiana later. Perhaps in August. With a sigh, he returned to his mother's letter.

Plans are underway for big changes in our fair city. Indiana is establishing a state public school system. Putnam County has sold the old County Seminary, established by John Thornburg in 1835, to Asbury University.

And elsewhere in town, the Greencastle Council decided to have wood-plank sidewalks built this spring and summer. They will connect the Square with the two new north and south railroad stations, and all the schools and churches. What a joy it will be to avoid sloshing through the mud!

Well, son, that's all the news from home. We look forward, as always, to hearing from you. Everyone here wants to say 'hello.'

Love,
Your Mother

Edward marveled at the changes in Greencastle his mother had depicted. Imagine, wooden sidewalks! What will they think of next?

* * *

August came and went, and Edward couldn't begin to think about returning to Greencastle. More and more he thought of Placerville as home. Life in California's Mother Lode was his reality. Indiana seemed far away, not only in distance, but also in his heart of hearts.

I'll just have to live with the feeling of guilt my mother's letters bring, he decided.

* * *

In February 1854, Thomas Springer surprised the Friday night supper-and-poker players with a hot-off-the-press edition of the *El Dorado Republican.*

"Look at this!" he announced. They gathered around, reading over his shoulders. *Newspaper to Change Hands! Springer and Cole Sell to Gelwicks and January.*

"You sold the paper?" Edward asked, bewildered. "But, why?"

"Dan, Dan Gelwicks that is, used to publish a newspaper in Coloma," Springer said. "He's moved to Placerville. He and Bill January wanted to buy me out, and keep the paper here. They plan to rename it the *Mountain Democrat.*"

"But, but…" Edward sputtered.

"But, what are *you* going to do?" asked Studebaker.

"I have absolutely no idea," Springer admitted. "They even bought the printing press—the first press in El Dorado County, I might add!"

"You don't know what you'll *do?"* Edward asked. "Not even a clue?"

"Well, I have some notions on the subject. I realize a town the size of Placerville probably couldn't support two papers. And Gelwicks made it condition of the bargain that I would not start a competing publication."

"So what are you thinking about?" asked Mark Hopkins.

"I'm not far enough along on that to say anything as yet," Springer replied, with a lifted eyebrow and a smile.

"Gelwicks and January will publish their first edition of the *Mountain Democrat* on February twenty-fifth," he added.

On May 13, 1854, a special issue of the *Mountain Democrat* reported the town's incorporation, retaining the name Placerville in preference to Ravine City, which was also suggested.

In a later edition, Edward read about Nebraska and Kansas having both been established as territories of the United States on May 30, 1854. He remembered crossing that area in 1850. The image was so clear; he could still feel and smell every inch of the prairie. What a wonderful part of the country it was!

* * *

Fall arrived.

Edward's mother's letters—liberally sprinkled with repeated hints and chiding—made it clear she wanted him to come home. *But,* Edward fumed, *I'm twenty-six years old. I should be allowed to live wherever I choose. Without feeling guilty*!

He realized his life in Placerville wasn't perfect. He still needed a wife. Rose and the other girls in the saloon were nice enough, but none were someone you'd marry.

He could just imagine introducing Rose to his family.

"And where did you two meet?"

"At the local brothel!"

That certainly wouldn't do! He wouldn't *have* to introduce her to his friends here. They would already know where they had met without a word being said. Would know exactly what she had been doing—and with whom.

But the fact he hadn't found a wife here didn't mean he had to return to Greencastle. It might be just as hard to find someone he wanted to marry *there.*

And, besides, it was way too late in the year to start a journey all the way across the continent. He had no choice but to stay. At least for now.

Chapter Forty-Three

Edward sat on the porch swing, protected from the cool breeze blowing down from the first snowfall in the High Sierras. The late October afternoon sun still warmed this, his favorite corner. Taking his mother's latest letter out of a pocket, he carefully broke the seal, and with pleased anticipation, began reading.

Dear Son,

I wish I could talk to you, face to face. Hold you in my arms as I tell you the sad news. It seems cold and unfeeling to simply write words on paper, to be sent miles across the continent, to be read by you, all by yourself, beyond my reach.

But, as I have no other choice, I shall write the words that are breaking my heart.

Eliza is dead.

Stunned, Edward stopped. Read the three words again, and yet again.

When comprehension came at last, with it came pain. Unimaginable pain.

It was as though someone had punched a fist into his stomach.

Clutching the letter, he stumbled across the porch and through the front door. Almost falling, he passed the parlor and dining room. He finally collapsed on a kitchen chair.

Eliza is dead.

The mental image came, of a fourteen-year-old girl, sitting at another kitchen table, explaining to ten-year-old Lawrence where California was. Eighteen forty-eight, and Edward had just read about the discovery of gold in California. How long ago it seemed.

Eliza is dead.

She's too young! Only twenty. Younger than he had been when, two years after that fondly remembered scene, he left Greencastle for California.

He forced himself to read on. Began the next sentence. *Your father's princess...*

A ghost of a smile came, in spite of his sorrow.

Father said his Grandmother Apphia claimed their family was directly descended from the great medieval king, Charlemagne. As a little girl, Eliza took that seriously. Making a crown out of Mother's necklace, she had held royal tea parties with her dolls.

And Father had taken to calling her "Princess."

Funny, he never referred to his sons as "Prince." It probably wasn't true, anyway. Couldn't be proven. But Great Grandmother Apphia *had* been adamant!

Edward returned to the letter.

Your father's princess is buried in Blackstock Cemetery on Hanna Street.

At the thought of his sister buried in the cold dark ground of a cemetery, Edward nearly threw up.

Swallowing hard, he finished the short letter.

Eliza came down with a fever and sore throat six days ago. She took to her bed. We called Dr. Samuels, of course. Father gave her Laudanum, while I brewed willow tea. Nothing helped. She simply grew weaker and weaker. In four days she was gone.

Our dear, sweet Eliza... gone.

Tears spilled down Edward's cheeks. Sobs, primeval in their rasping sound, echoed through the house.

He laid his head on folded arms on the kitchen table and surrendered himself to the pain and loss.

Later—the room was now dark—he blew his nose, pumped water into the basin on the sink, and rinsed the tears from his face.

Returning to his seat, he pondered. If he had known, just a month earlier, he could have returned to Greencastle this fall. But, now it was too late.

He should have been there to comfort his parents—and be comforted in return. And Lawrence! Just sixteen. An awkward age under any circumstances, but to lose his big sister, and be left the only child at home. What could be sadder? Or harder to bear?

"Why, God?" he asked out loud. "Why Eliza? Why not me?"

The spoken words only served to emphasize the ensuing silence.

Chapter Forty-Four

The next morning, Edward stood at the door of the post office. Although he'd never been drunk in his life, he felt as if he had a hangover. A bad one.

His swollen eyes felt gritty. The sun pierced them as if the light had broken into tiny shards of glass. His head pounded. The dirty wooden step looked like a fine place to curl up in a ball and sleep. Goodness knows, he'd not slept at all the night before.

It took all the strength he could muster to pull the door.

"You look like hell," Nugent said, looking up. "What happened?"

"Nothing."

"Well, *something's* wrong."

"I *don't* want to talk about it!"

Nugent looked perplexed—and wounded.

Edward felt a stab of remorse, but could do nothing about it. If he allowed himself to even think about...

He closed his eyes, trying not to break into tears.

If he cried any more...

He had a sudden image of his eyeballs dissolving into blobs of blue running down his face.

“Have it your own way,” Nugent muttered, and returned to sorting mail.

Edward shuffled to his place behind the counter; opened another mailbag. Just then the door opened. Miners began arriving to send letters home and pick up their mail.

Fortunately, Edward could do all that was required without thinking. The routine job was enough to keep his thoughts away from his mother’s letter, barely. Images of Eliza floated, ghostlike, around the edges of his consciousness. Resolutely, he weighed gold dust, handed out letters, and sorted mail.

❋ ❋ ❋

As the sun was setting, Nugent turned the sign to CLOSED and locked the door.

“Alright, you’ve moped around here all day. Now sit,” he indicated the bench along one wall, “and start talking.”

Edward sighed. Too exhausted to protest, he did as he was ordered. Sat. Took a deep breath.

Nugent sat next to him, waiting quietly.

“My…” Edward’s voice cracked. “My sister…” He closed his eyes. Saw her face. “She’s… she’s dead.”

“Oh,” Nugent sighed. “I am *so sorry*. Was that in the letter you picked up yesterday?”

“Yes.”

“She was younger than you, right?”

"Yes. Just twenty. Going to be a schoolteacher. Unless she got..." Edward choked. Shook his head. "Now she'll..." he swallowed, "*never* get married."

"Sad as it is, people *do* die," Nugent said quietly.

Images passed through Edward's mind. Four-year-old Caleb. Gould. Cousin George. Cousin John. Eliza. All innocents. Good people.

"But, why them and not me?" Edward shook his head again. "I've done whatever I pleased. Left home and didn't go back when I had the chance." He paused. "If I'd been there, maybe Eliza wouldn't have died."

"There's probably nothing you could have done. It was just God's will."

Edward sat up, his eyes blazing. "How could a *just* God kill good people? How could He decide Eliza should die?"

"I don't know," Nugent admitted. "We, as a people, gave up our right to live forever, back in the Garden of Eden. I guess the best we can hope for, is the knowledge that the Bible tells us, we don't die forever. Eliza's in heaven, with your two young cousins."

"I used to believe that." Edward sat silently wrestling with his turbulent thoughts. "But, right now," his voice dropped to a mere whisper, "I can't even believe there *is* a God."

"Pray," Nugent urged. "He's here, waiting and listening."

"I tried to pray all last night. But I couldn't feel anything. It was like throwing a pebble into a pond, but there wasn't any splash. No rings of water moving out from where the pebble had fallen. Nothing."

"How long has it been since you've been to church?"

Edward thought, trying to remember. "Not since Fort Laramie, I guess."

"You've never gone to church since you've been here?"

"In case you haven't noticed, I work Sundays!"

Nugent looked somewhat startled, then smiled. "I guess we'll have to change that. Starting tomorrow, you're to go to church in the morning, and report for work after dinner, at two o'clock."

"And if I don't go to church?"

"You won't have a job."

Edward frowned. "You'd *fire* me for not going to church?"

"You bet!"

"But, but how would you know whether I went or not?"

Nugent smiled. "Because I'd *look* for you."

"You're going to church, too? Who'll take care of the post office?"

"I just decided to close the post office on Sunday mornings."

"You're closing on Sunday mornings to make *me* go to church?"

"No. So *everyone* can go to church if they want. They can get their mail Sunday afternoon. Or Saturday. Or any other day of the week."

Edward frowned. "Why do *you* care whether or not *I* go to church?"

Nugent smiled. Laid a hand on Edward's shoulder. "I care that your prayers go 'splash.'"

Chapter Forty-Five

As Edward pulled the church door open, the sound of singing accompanied by an out-of-tune piano swept over him.

A mighty fortress is our God,
A bulwark never failing;
Our helper He, amid the flood
Of mortal ills prevailing.

He nearly slammed the door shut and returned home. What was he doing there? He didn't belong. God had abandoned him. And, Eliza was dead.

For still our ancient foe
Doth seek to work us woe;
His craft and pow'r are great,
And arm'd with cruel hate,
On earth is not his equal.

He thought of Nugent, sitting in church, expecting him to attend. Gritting his teeth, Edward walked through the doorway and slunk to a seat in the back.

After a rustling as the congregation sat again on their benches, expectant silence replaced sound. The preacher, in his black suit, white shirt, and black string tie, walked to the pulpit and spread his arms. "Brothers and sisters, *This is the day the Lord has made; let us rejoice and be glad in it."* He lowered his arms. "The words of Psalm one hundred eighteen, verse twenty-four. And we *do* thank God for his many blessings."

A loud voice rang out. *"How can I rejoice and be glad, when Eliza is dead. When God let her die?"*

A rustle of people turning, then shocked silence followed by murmured whispers. Edward realized everyone had turned to stare at him. He was standing. The loud voice had been his!

The preacher paused. Looked around the congregation. Looked at him. Said nothing. The silence became tangible.

Then the preacher said, "But what about the times when we pray? Pray hard? And hear—" another long pause, then softly, "silence?"

Edward returned the preacher's penetrating stare. "How do you know what I was thinking?" he asked, his voice beyond his control. He felt a strong urge to get up, then and there, and walk out of the church. Run as far away as possible. But, he couldn't move.

"I know," replied the preacher, "because, ladies and gentlemen, children of the congregation, I believe that on this day, in this very place, we are witnessing a miracle. A miracle of the Holy Spirit at work in our lives.

"What is your name, young man?" he asked.

"E...Ed...Edward. Edward D...Dain...Daingerfield."

Acting as if there was no one else in the church, the preacher asked quietly, "Who is it, Edward, that has died?"

"Eliza. My sister. Back home. In Greencastle, Indiana."

"How old was your sister, Eliza?"

"Only twenty. She was going to be a teacher. But... but..."

"Only twenty," the preacher echoed Edward's words.

Then, his eyes sweeping the congregation, he continued in a conversational tone, "Until last Friday night, I was planning to deliver an entirely different sermon this morning. But, that night, I knew I needed to prepare this sermon—for this Sunday. Knew someone needed to hear these words—today.

"I believe the Holy Spirit is working through me to comfort our brother, Edward." He turned once again. "Edward, have you ever attended this church before?"

"No, sir."

"I thought not."

"Why did you come this morning?"

"Because my boss, Nugent, at the post office, told me he'd fire me if I didn't come."

A titter of laughter from the congregation greeted this statement.

"He even said he would close the post office *every* Sunday morning, so I wouldn't have to work. Wouldn't have an excuse not to come to church." He paused. "He said he'd close it so *everybody* could come to church and pick up their mail some other time."

The preacher's eyes searched the congregation, lighting on Nugent. "Brother Nugent, did the Holy Spirit speak to you?"

"I don't think so, sir," Nugent answered. "Only Edward."

"Well, I'm convinced it did. Perhaps it was through the words and actions of Brother Edward, here. But, the Holy Spirit works in mysterious ways, its wonders to perform."

The preacher turned to sweep the entire congregation in his gaze. "And this day, the Holy Spirit is here, in this church. Inspiring this sermon."

"We can pray!" the preacher's voice thundered, making everyone jump. "Pray hard." His voice dropped to a whisper. "And hear—silence. It's hard to live with silence, especially from God."

Edward sat, hanging on every word.

"We can be experiencing hard times," the preacher continued. "We ask God, why this? Why him? Why her? Why me? And all we hear is—silence."

"But, why *was* it her? Why my sweet Eliza?" It wasn't until the congregation turned to look at him, that Edward realized he'd spoken the questions out loud.

The preacher smiled. Indicated with a gesture, to wait. Then continued, "But we must acknowledge, it is only God's *occasional* silence we must endure.

"We have all witnessed miracles. Prayers answered."

The preacher took a sip of water from the glass on the pulpit. "Beware, my friends," he paused, nodded his head slowly, "God's silence can lead to loss of faith. To questioning God's very existence!"

Edward felt like trying to hide. Wanted to crawl under the bench. Even though the pastor's eyes scanned over everyone in the congregation, Edward *knew* the man was talking directly to him.

"What can we do when God is silent? Open your Bibles to Psalm twenty-two, verse one. The words of David:

My God, my God, why hast thou forsaken me?
Why art thou so far from me,
and from the words of my roaring?
O my God, I cry in the daytime, but thou hearest not;
and in the night season, and am not silent.

And again, Jesus cried out from the cross,

My God, my God, why hast thou forsaken me?

"There are many places in the Bible, where David and others have questioned God. Wondered why they felt abandoned by Him. But then, in contrast, we come to Psalm twenty-three,

The Lord is my shepherd; I shall not want.

And even more strongly, Psalm one hundred thirty-nine,

Where can I go from your spirit?
Where can I flee from your presence?

"Yes, my friends, God is only *occasionally* silent. We have proof in the Bible, both of God's presence, and of his absence. Therefore, God's silence shouldn't surprise us. We should *expect* it.

"Paradoxically enough, God's silence can bring us closer to Him."

By now, Edward was so completely comfortable talking to the preacher, out loud, in the middle of the sermon, he asked, "How can *that* be?"

A gentle smile lit the preacher's face. "We won't always understand the reasons for God's silence. But remember the words of Isaiah; *God's ways are not our ways.* When we don't understand God's silences, remember, we weren't meant to."

"That's not much help," Edward said, defiance making him stubborn.

"What can we do when faced with God's silence? When we are filled with doubt?" the preacher replied.

"*That* doubt is the work of the *evil* one. *We* must remain strong, and remember the faith of the Twenty-third Psalm. True faith is holding on to God—even when we don't understand. Even in his silences. After all, God *trusts* us with his silence. He has *faith* in us. Faith that we can handle his silences.

"What can we do when tested by His silence? Continue our part in the dialogue. Pray. After all, what else *can* we do? Where else can we go, but to God? Go to God and remember His faithfulness. Immediately after expressing hurt and frustration in God's silence, David says,

Our fathers trusted in thee;
they trusted, and thou didst deliver them.
They cried unto thee, and were delivered;
they trusted in thee, and were not confounded.

"In the midst of hard times," the preacher reminded them, "God's silence determines how deep our faith is. In the midst of God's silence—that's when our faith can grow the most.

"What can you do when you are tempted to doubt God? Think of the sun. Do you believe there is a sun, even when it's not shining? Do you believe there is such a thing as love, even when you don't feel loved? Well then, believe in God—even when he is silent.

"Let us kneel in prayer."

Edward kneeled. Bowed his head, his thoughts racing. *Was it the Holy Spirit that brought me here? That inspired the preacher to give this sermon today? It must have been. There's no other explanation. I only told Nugent about Eliza's death, my doubts, last night after the post office was closed.*

I can only believe I was led by God—perhaps through Nugent, perhaps through Eliza's death—to this place. Led to hear this sermon. Led back to Him.

The out-of-tune piano began to play. People stood. They sang.

O God, our help in ages past,
Our hope for years to come,
Our shelter from the stormy blast,
And our eternal home.

Edward had never heard anything more beautiful.

Chapter Forty-Six

While waiting to speak to Nugent—who certainly knew he'd attended church—Edward saw Thomas Springer, the former owner of the *Mountain Democrat,* coming down the aisle.

"Well, well," Springer said, "Nugent let you out of the post office long enough to attend church, did he?" He smiled and clapped his friend on the back. "I'm sorry for your loss, but this was one of the most exciting mornings I've ever experienced. At least in church!

"My dear," Nugent addressed the lady next to him, "this is Edward Brochenbrough Daingerfield, 'E.B.' to his friends. He works in the post office, drives the stage, and goodness knows what else.

"E.B., this is my wife, Mary."

"How do you do, Mrs. Springer," Edward reached out, tentatively took her hand, and nodded. "I'm very happy to meet you."

"And this," Springer nodded in the direction of a young boy, holding tight to his mother's skirt, "is our five-year-old son, Grant."

"I'm very happy to meet you, young man," Edward said, gravely shaking the small hand.

"You talked out loud in church," the boy said, his face filled with wonder.

"Yes, I did," Edward admitted. "Though, I don't think I'd recommend doing it again."

"And, as you can no doubt see," Springer quickly changed the topic of conversation, "we are soon to have another child in the family."

"Congratulations. I hope all goes well with you and the baby," Edward said.

"Thank you." Mary Springer smiled and blushed slightly. "I don't know why Thomas hasn't brought you to our home," she looked at her husband with mock dismay, "but you must come to dinner some Sunday after church."

"It would be my pleasure, Ma'am, I'm sure."

How strange, Edward thought, *this feels just like any Sunday in Greencastle—families greeting each other, inviting, and being invited, to dinner. Somehow, I never thought of Springer as being married, having a small child. Most of the people I've met here have been single men. Or at least, I assumed they were single. The only women I've come into contact with are 'upstairs ladies.' Not like Mrs. Springer, who's just like any lady from home.*

Edward looked around the church. He noted most seemed to be families. This was an entirely different society in Placerville, one he hadn't even been aware of. He smiled. *I must come to church more often. Surely, some of these ladies aren't married.*

❊ ❊ ❊

Spring, 1855

"E.B., I've got a proposition for you."

Edward sat at the Springer's dining room table. Mary was taking the remains of Sunday dinner back to the kitchen. One-year-old Thomas Junior sat in his high chair, banging on the wooden tray with a spoon. Meanwhile, Grant, now a robust six-year-old, was playing on the floor with a wooden replica of a stagecoach Edward had given him as a birthday gift.

"And what might that be? Your proposition."

"I've been approached by people from Volcano, urging me to get back into the newspaper business. And, since you had newspaper experience back in Indiana, I wondered if you'd be interested in joining me as a partner in the business."

"Whew!" Edward sat back in his chair, feeling stunned. "I... I don't know what to say."

"You don't have to say anything just yet. It's only an idea. But, you might like to think about it.

"Here's the deal," Springer looked serious. "Placerville already has the newspaper I sold to Gelwicks and January, and the town can't support two. Most of the other towns in the Mother Lode already have their own papers; Jackson has the *Sentinel.* Quincy, Muletown and Augusta are smaller, but they've got the *Quincy Prospector.*

"I know you're acquainted with Sutter Creek and Jackson, from your stagecoach route, but have you ever been to Volcano?"

Edward mentally pictured the area, and then shook his head. "Nope. In Jackson, I've left off mail bags for Volcano, and picked up freight, but I've never, personally, been there

"It's getting to be a really nice town. Miners have poured in by the thousands. They've got… let me check my list, here…" Springer took a piece of paper out of his pocket. "forty-seven saloons, two breweries—"

"That sounds like a lovely town to raise two children," Mary Springer interrupted, as she returned from the kitchen and took the baby out of his highchair and onto her lap. "We really need to live in a town with forty-seven saloons and two breweries!"

"But, my dear, it also has twelve restaurants, five hotels, any number of stores, *and* a church. They're building a theater and planning to form a theatre group—the first in the state! I've heard plans for a rental library—also the first in the state—so Volcano's citizens don't lack for culture." Springer gave his wife a 'so there' look. "At least *some* of them can read!"

Mary smiled her acceptance of his research.

"And Volcano's leaders are plotting to take the County Seat away from Jackson. As part of their campaign, they'll see to it the paper's profitable."

Edward sat, listening to them, his mind in a daze. *Newspaper? Volcano?*

"There are a couple of drawbacks for you," Springer turned to Edward. "First, of course, we'd have to move to Volcano. And second, there'd be expenses in setting up a newspaper office, especially since I sold the printing press to Gelwicks and January.

"And... I know you have a home here, and so do we... but," he put his elbows on the table and looked earnestly at Edward, "our houses could be collateral for the business, and I've located a press we could purchase and move to Volcano pretty reasonably."

"You're serious about this," Edward said, amazed. "I mean," he paused, "you've really looked into it. Counted the saloons and hotels, calculated the possible market for a newspaper, the costs, everything!"

Springer nodded. Sat back. Cocked an eyebrow, inviting Edward's response.

"I... I don't know what to say. I'm flabbergasted!"

"You don't have to say anything today. Take some time to think about it. But don't take too long. Mary and I have talked it over, and we're definitely going to do it.

"And, I don't know if you've ever met him, but a good friend of mine," he shrugged his shoulders, "ours—the Honorable P.C. Johnson, is going to join us. He's a lawyer, but mostly does literary matters associated with the law. He's a brilliant writer, and I'm a *brilliant* printer." Springer smiled modestly, but not for a moment belittling his pride. "You've had experience in gathering and writing the news, and distribution, too. So I think we'd make a great team."

Edward swallowed. Thought, *my beautiful house, the post office, my stagecoach route, Wednesday lunches at Nancy's... Am I ready to give all that up?*

"I'll think about your proposal." He paused, trying to clear his head. "Thank you, for even considering me. But, I don't know if I'm ready for such a big move."

Chapter Forty-Seven

October 1855

Once Edward had made his decision, it was amazing how quickly everything happened.

"So you're up and leaving Placerville?" asked Nugent. "Quitting the post office, driving stage."

"I suppose it was bound to happen," Edward responded. He grinned wryly. "I quit school and came to California. Stopped mining for gold and went to work for the post office. Then I added becoming a teamster.

"With such a sterling record, why wouldn't I just pack up and leave everything to become co-owner of a newspaper?"

"What about your house?"

"I offered to rent it to Jack Brown. You know Mrs. Brown, Edna, has been cleaning and cooking for me, since I moved in. They seemed really pleased to pay rent to live in the house."

Nugent grunted and said, "Well, I won't hold your job open for you, but feel welcome to come see me when you decide to give up being a newspaper man and come back to Placerville."

* * *

By October, Edward and Springer had rented a room in the Hanford and Downs' "Eagle" building. It headed Consolation Street, on the west side of Main in Volcano. The newspaper office and printing press were located next to a "fashionable" billiard saloon on the second floor. Their entire room was only 16 by 20 feet.

Springer and his wife obtained a house for their family, and rented a bedroom to P.C. Johnson. Edward rented a room in a boarding house.

While Springer went over their press with a fine-tooth comb to be sure it would be up to the job of printing the weekly paper, Edward introduced himself to the town of Volcano.

"Good morning," he'd say, handing the proprietor a business card. "My name is Edward Brochenbrough Daingerfield. My friends call me E.B. We, Thomas Springer, P.C. Johnson, and I, are starting a weekly newspaper in Volcano. We'd be happy to print up a suitable advertisement for your establishment for a very reasonable price. And if you have any special events, we'll make every effort to include the details in our news stories, at no cost to you, of course."

Normally somewhat shy with strangers, Edward had no trouble talking to anyone and everyone as a representative of the *Volcano Weekly Ledger*. As a matter of fact, he thoroughly enjoyed playing that role.

He learned the Methodist Church was having a box-lunch social and wrote an appropriate story. He talked to a Mrs.

Lucille Walker, recently arrived from England, and proud owner of a cozy bed-and-breakfast. She was thinking of serving tea there.

"Not a stiff and formal tea, my dear boy," she said. "No, not at all formal. I'm picturing more of a genteel afternoon tea for ladies and gentlemen, and open to families with well-behaved children, don't you know.

"I might start out with Saturday afternoons, just to see what the reception is. Then, if there's sufficient interest, I shall expand the tea to other days of the week."

Edward promised to write a story about her venture, for which he received a genteel pat on the cheek.

He also received orders for advertisement from nearly every store, hotel, and other business in Volcano.

While Johnson penned his essays, Edward designed advertisements and wrote up everything he'd heard about local events.

He was very proud of his opening editorial when the first edition of the *Ledger* came out on Saturday, October 27, 1855.

The Initial Bow

It is a common custom when an individual assumes the responsible position of conducting a newspaper that he should, in a measure, state the course which he intends to pursue in the discharge of that duty.

When we first proposed to establish the Ledger, *we assured this community that it would be a strictly neutral paper as far as politics of the day were concerned. We have not changed our mind on the subject. The people who compose the great political parties of the day, we believe to be alike honest and patriotic in all their feelings and actions, and that each have the common good of the country at heart. An honest difference of opinion as to the best means to accomplish this should be regarded with kind consideration.*

It will be the aim of the Ledger *to guard carefully the interests of Volcano, and her inhabitants, not neglecting those who live in the country surrounding us. Where the rights and privileges of our citizens are in danger of being assailed and trampled upon, we will speak freely and without fear; and we will hold up to public censure the wrongdoings with the same good will that we would chronicle the acts of the good and deserving. We will endeavor to give all the local as well as foreign news of the day, in as condensed and concise form as possible. We promise nothing more—but set our little craft before the breeze, hoping she may not be wrecked upon the breakers of public opinion."*

The next day, Springer said, "You'd best get yourself to Coloma as quickly as possible. They're hanging Mickey Free and Jerry Crane at Sutter's Sawmill, day after tomorrow. You need to get the whole story for next week's edition!"

Chapter Forty-Eight

Edward realized the hanging was going to be big news when he encountered people walking or riding in wagons, carts, and every other means of conveyance while he was still some distance from Coloma. There wasn't a bed available anywhere in town, and they were even running out of food to feed the crowd.

Fortunately, Nancy cheerfully agreed to let him to sleep in her spare bedroom. And she'd provide him what food she had.

"I don't promise it be much," she admitted. "We can eat what Peter's grown in the vegetable garden. I 'spect he need keep watch over the patch, else somebody come steal what he growed."

"Anything you can manage is fine with me." Edward looked out the window at the hordes of people roaming up and down the street outside. "I've never seen so many people."

"They all come to watch the hangin'. I 'spect that's why you come, too."

"I'm editor of the Volano newspaper now, and writing an article about the hanging. I've got to admit, I've never witnessed anything like this. Not at all sure I want to. And even less sure I want to write about it for others to read."

Nancy nodded in mute agreement.

"Well," Edward sighed, "I guess I'd best get out into the fray and see what I can find out about the two criminals."

❈ ❈ ❈

Edward walked through the crush of bodies to the post office. "Good to see you again, Jim," he said, shaking the postmaster's hand. "I'm writing up the hangings for the Volcano paper. Anything you can tell me about those two?"

"This is the biggest thing to hit Coloma since the discovery of gold!" the postmaster said, shaking his head in wonder.

"Were the two of them in cahoots?"

"Nope. Two different men. Two different crimes. Both murderers, but no other similarity between them."

The postmaster shuffled through several sheets of paper. "There's 'wanted' posters and information in here somewhere," he muttered. "Ah, here it is."

Edward scanned the sheets... *"Mickey Free... born in Brockford, Canada... committed his first theft at age ten... stole a pair of rabbits... fined and sentenced to thirty days imprisonment."*

He looked up. "Nice kid!"

"One of the best," Jim agreed, tongue in cheek.

Edward read on. *"Second offense... stole six or seven shillings from an old lady..."* He looked up, amazed, *"while they were both in church!"*

He looked down again and continued, *"Robbed a Brockford store, twice... went to Chicago, committing numerous thefts along the way... stole fifty dollars from a wealthy woman... committed several other thefts on Mississippi steamboats.*

"It says here, *Free arrived in San Francisco, destitute.* What'd he do with all the stolen money?"

The postmaster shrugged his shoulders. "Beats me."

"I guess I won't mind watching such an habitual criminal hang. But, I'm still not sure I want to write about it for the paper. Do you really think people want to read stuff like this?"

"Look outside. All those people came to see it first hand. My guess is everybody in the state will be wanting to read all the gory details."

"May I borrow these papers? That is, if you don't need them right now. I can use the information to start the background for the story."

"You're welcome to borrow them, but I would like them back. Someday, they could be worth something."

"I'll bring them back tomorrow."

* * *

Back in Nancy and Peter Gooch's guest room, Edward read the rest of the Free's story.

Winding up in Mud Spring, Mickey Free, George Wilson, and Stewart Kelly, a New Yorker, said to be of a decent family, made a business of robbing Chinese camps. Wilson, the brains of the gang, was a "Sydney Duck" (slang for Australian ex-convict).

They robbed, and then shot two men—D.S. Howe and his partner—who kept a roadhouse and trading post at Slippery Ford. After the shooting, Kelly cut their throats, though he testified that Wilson and Free compelled him to do it.

The constable of White Oak Township arrested George Wilson and Mickey Free. When they came to trial, Wilson turned state's evidence, which helped convict Free. In return Wilson wasn't prosecuted.

So now, Mickey Free awaits hanging here, in Coloma, Edward mused.

Edward strolled into the kitchen. "Hey Nancy, do you suppose White Oak Township's constable is here in Coloma?"

"Honey, everyone in California's here in Coloma!"

* * *

He found the constable standing in front of Coloma's jail, leaning against the wall, arms folded across his chest. A crowd had gathered to hear his story. Edward took out a pad of paper and started taking notes.

"Kelly wasn't tried here at Coloma," the constable was saying. "I arrested him in Napa County. Then he got a change of venue to Sacramento County. After the trial, in May 1856, the judge sentenced him to be hanged. His buddy, Wilson, was the chief witness against him.

"I guess we'll get to see the end of him tomorrow."

* * *

Tucking his notes into a back pocket, Edward made his way back to his room, to read about the other man to be hanged, Jeremiah Crane.

The information Jim had loaned him said, *Jeremiah Crane, a resident of Ring Gold in El Dorado County, and a schoolmaster there, was convicted of murdering Susan M. Newnham—one of his students!*

Crane, over thirty years old, claimed he was in love with Miss Newnham, and married to her. But, he confessed, not in any church ceremony, since he already had a wife and four children living near Lexington, Kentucky.

Edward looked up. Swallowed. The man had to be crazy!

Crane shot the girl with his Colt's revolver on August tenth. She survived until the fifteenth. Before she died, she said Crane hadn't forced her to "sing" the oath of marriage, but just "worried it out of her."

When Crane was arrested, a large crowd gathered to lynch him. With great difficulty, Sheriff Dave Buel saved the murderer, put him on a horse, and took him to jail in Coloma.

Edward lay on the bed, hands behind his head, letting his mind wander. This was not like writing up box lunch socials or genteel teas at the bed-and-breakfast! What was the world coming to?

* * *

Friday, October twenty-sixth, dawned clear and bright. Edward joined the five or six thousand people who gathered to witness the event. They stood or sat in wagons covering the hills around a small ravine where the gallows had been built. Edward knew why *he* was here, covering the hangings for the newspaper, but it amazed him to see so many women and whole families gathered there to watch.

Having never seen anything like a hanging, he didn't know what to expect, but the doomed prisoners' behavior seemed very strange. First, Crane gave a rambling forty-five minute speech, the burden of which was, "the Bible is a fable."

Free didn't make a speech. He started to sing a song, but stopped when he forgot the words. Then he tried to dance a jig, but it was a pretty lame performance.

The prisoners then sang a duet, composed by Crane for the occasion, while Edward hurriedly scribbled the words on his notepad.

Come friends and all others I bid you adieu
The gates are now open to welcome us through.
No valleys or shadow do I see on the road
For the angels are waiting to take me to God.
My body no longer my spirit shall claim
This day I am going from sorrow and pain.
The necklace and gallows will soon set me free
Where all love each other and ever agree.
I am going, I am going, I am going, I am gone.
Oh friends and relations, it is done; it is done.

Edward marveled at how orderly and quiet the crowds were. He gave full credit to Sheriff Carson and his deputies.

* * *

As Edward would later write in his article for the *Ledger, After a short prayer was offered, the final preparations were completed, and at twenty minutes before two o'clock, the prisoners were launched into eternity. With the fall of the block, both necks were broken, and they died without a struggle.*

Crane had friends who took his body to Ring Gold for interment. Mickey Free was buried at the foot of the gallows.

⁜ ⁜ ⁜

But now, Edward stood crushed in the crowd of silent, clearly shocked people. The frenzied energy that had carried him through yesterday and today drained away, leaving him weak-kneed.

He wondered idly, how many people might read his article in the *Volcano Ledger.* Hundreds? He mentally shrugged. If he sent a copy to *The Argus,* what would his family—and the other good citizens of Greencastle—think about witnessing a hanging? About living where two such barbaric, unrepentant murderers could exist?

Whatever happened, Edward knew this was a day *he* would remember for as long as he lived. He just hoped the sight of those two bodies dangling at the ends of ropes wouldn't haunt his dreams equally long.

Chapter Forty-Nine

The first week in November, Springer told Edward about the Christmas Ball to be held in Volcano.

"I'm head of the committee for arrangements," he said, "and we'll need to give it plenty of publicity."

"All right," Edward agreed. "Tell me who, what, why, where, when."

"On Christmas evening, at Mahoney Hall, here in Volcano. I expect you to be there. You *do* know a nice lady to invite, don't you?"

Edward shrugged. "The only 'lady' I know, besides your wife, is Caroline Gould."

"The one with the boarding house in Sacramento?"

"Yes."

"Well, invite *her*. But do it soon. That time of year, especially Christmas Day, people make engagements months in advance."

"The only thing is..." Edward hesitated.

"Yes?"

"She might not want to leave her daughter in boarding school, all by herself, on Christmas Day."

"How old is the daughter?"

"She's only fifteen."

"Hmmm," Springer mused. "That might not be too young."

"What do you mean?"

"Invite the daughter, too." At Edward's incredulous look, Springer continued. "She's old enough to dance. I'm sure her boarding school has taught her the social graces. And there's always a need for extra females."

"But, a fifteen-year-old at a Christmas Ball?"

"This is going to be a nice occasion. Don't forget I was an officer of the Placerville division of the Sons of Temperance. While I can't force my strongly-held convictions on everyone else, and there might be champagne for the midnight supper, I can guarantee you, it won't be anything like the Saturnalia they held in Rich Bar four years ago."

"From what I heard of *that* event," Edward said, "they started on Christmas Eve and continued, nearly non-stop through most of January."

"You heard right," Springer answered. "Of course, that celebration had nothing to do with any Christian holiday. They copied Roman orgies of ancient days. Mules brought in casks of brandy and baskets of champagne. The celebration began with a lantern-lit parade, led by The General with his tremendous snow-white beard. Great toasts, orations and musical crooning accompanied the oyster and champagne supper. Afterward, they danced all night and into the next, until the dancers fell in drunken heaps.

"While we may dance all night, it will not continue into the next," Springer promised, "and *no one* will become part of a drunken heap!"

"Well, I know Caroline wouldn't approve of Ellen being exposed to excessive drinking," Edward said. "But, still, isn't fifteen a bit young to be dancing with grownups?"

"Why don't you invite them both, and see what her mother says. At least, she'll be there to chaperone. And, if it makes any difference, we can double-up the boys, and invite your two guests to stay overnight at our house, rather than one of the hotels."

"Well," Edward finally agreed, "I can invite them and see what Caroline decides."

❊ ❊ ❊

On Christmas evening, a proud Edward entered Mahoney Hall with Caroline on one arm and Ellen on the other. They stopped just inside the door to look in amazement at the decorations. Bows and swags of red and white calico provided a bright contrast to sprays of evergreens. Candles burned and sparkled, turning the huge room into a forest wonderland.

An orchestra, two fiddle players, an accordion, and bass, sat on a raised dais, playing Christmas carols while the guests visited, nibbled finger sandwiches, and sipped apple cider.

When the music changed to a dance tune, Edward bowed before Caroline for the first dance. She smiled. Nodded. And took his hand. Walking out to the center of the dance floor, Edward thought about their relationship. Neither of them was married. She was only ten years older than he, and good company. They had shared so much.

They waltzed around the floor, surrounded by other dancing couples. She felt good in his arms. For years he had longed for a woman. A wife. Could *she* be the one? They were certainly comfortable together. They had friendship and mutual respect. She smiled, humming to the music.

Returning her to a seat, he noticed what a good-looking woman she was, her curls piled on top of her head, her brown eyes shining. He returned her smile as she sat.

Another man brought Ellen back to sit next to Caroline. Edward turned and asked Ellen for the second dance. She nodded and grinned. "Oh, yes!"

As the music began, he held out his hand. She took it, like a princess. Together they walked to the dance floor.

As they started to dance, he felt a strange sensation. He stepped back, looking at her closely as she twirled out and back again. His heart nearly stopped!

Where was little Ellen? The schoolgirl? The child? Dressed in peach, with lace ruffles at throat and wrists, she was a vision of elegance. Her light brown curls cascaded from a large, peach satin bow.

He felt his face flush. Her body felt so right in his arms. *But, I can't love you! You're only fifteen. I'm twenty-seven. Ellen*, he thought, *you're all grown up! And I don't know what to do about it.* He realized he couldn't let either Ellen or Caroline know how he felt.

He asked Mary Springer for the next dance, wondering if inappropriate feelings would well up with her as well. Perhaps he'd suddenly been cursed with some strange malady. But, they simply enjoyed the sociability of the music, the dance, and each other's company. Feeling somewhat light-headed, he realized he *could* act normally with a woman in his arms. They were only dancing. He sighed with relief!

He asked the widow Walker of the Bed and Breakfast for a dance. She was plump and pink-cheeked, and thoroughly enjoying the genteel entertainment for ladies and gentlemen. "Perhaps," she chirped, "we should have monthly tea dances. They're all the rage in London."

Not knowing whether he could survive another encounter with the mixed feelings she engendered, he asked Caroline for a dance. She was his guest, after all, so he couldn't ignore her.

Taking their place on the dance floor, Caroline's eyes twinkled as she gave him a 'we've-got-a-secret' kind of smile that nearly broke Edward's heart. With a feeling of guilt, he thought, *she obviously felt my reaction to our first dance together. She's a dear friend. But how do I let her know that's all I feel for her. How do I tell her I simply can't consider marrying her?*

Caroline was so obviously enjoying the evening and the dance, Edward decided to do likewise and postpone any discussion of their future for another day.

Just before the midnight supper, Edward danced again with Ellen. She blossomed like a bud suddenly turning into a full-blown rose as he placed his hand at her waist. *Oh, Ellen, Ellen, my sweet child, you are so young and naïve. Inexperienced in the world of men and women, you couldn't begin to understand what I'm feeling for you.*

He took a deep breath and smiled at his eager partner. He simply had to rein in his unhealthy feelings and help her enjoy her first grown-up ball.

When they danced a Virginia reel, Edward felt his tension relax. This was a musical play-party game rather than an adult partner dance. Going through the various patterns he could enjoy the boisterous romp.

They took their seats, Caroline on one side, Ellen on the other, for the first course of the Champagne-and-oysters midnight supper. Conscious of Tom Springer's opposition to alcoholic beverages, and Ellen's tender age, their group drank only apple cider. Edward was actually relieved. He needed to keep his wits about him to control his words and actions.

As the evening came to an end, he walked Caroline and Ellen back to the Springer's home. He loved them both. Marriage with Caroline would have been quite appropriate, but he had to face the fact that his feelings for her were insufficient to warrant a marriage. Yet, he couldn't bear to break his friend's heart if she actually felt a romantic attachment. *How can I possibly tell you, 'I can't marry you because I love your daughter?'*

And to declare my love for a fifteen-year-old child should land me in jail!

Oh, God. What am I going to do?

Chapter Fifty

Overcome with guilt and confusion, Edward wished he could confide in someone. But that was out of the question.

True, he attended the Methodist Church with Springer and his family, but he didn't feel confident enough to talk to the preacher about something as personal as his desire (or was it lust?) for a child who had just turned sixteen on January ninth. He certainly couldn't talk to his partner. Springer was well married, to a completely suitable wife, and would only shake his head in disgust, if he were told.

Edward wished his cousin Richard and friend Louis, were still in California. They'd heckle him, then start throwing punches, until they were all bloody and exhausted. Perhaps that was what he needed to knock the ridiculous notion right out of his head.

A couple of weeks into January, Caroline sent Edward an invitation to come to dinner at her boarding house. Ellen would be safely back at school. But, what of Caroline? What would he do if she entertained thoughts of love and marriage? What *could* he do?

They had been friends, practically forever. She'd think it strange if he suddenly started avoiding her.

Edward's schedule was pretty routine by now. Monday through Wednesday he wrote up articles and ads for the paper, going out to do interviews if necessary. As soon as each was written, he'd hand it over to Springer, who started setting the type. Thursday and Friday, Springer printed up the papers, and wanted Edward out from underfoot.

Each Saturday, Edward donned his navy blue uniform with bright brass buttons, to deliver the paper to every business and home subscriber. He used this opportunity to solicit new ads and gather information for the next week's edition. Handing out newspapers with his and Springer's names on the masthead, he felt a sense of elation.

Volcano Weekly Ledger

PUBLISHED EVERY SATURDAY, BY:

T.A. Springer & Company

T.A. Springer E.B. Daingerfield

With no little foreboding, he replied to Caroline's invitation. He would be delighted to come to dinner at noon the following Thursday.

* * *

Caroline greeted him at the door with a proud smile and proprietary air, wrapped her hand around his arm, and led him into the dining room.

"This is our Edward Daingerfield," she announced to those seated at the long table.

Edward could feel his face heat. "Nice to meet you," he said to the new residents. "Good to see you again, sir," as he shook hands with those he'd met at the boarding house before.

As Caroline passed around platters of fried fish, sliced roast beef, potatoes and gravy, green beans, and cabbage, she mentioned the Christmas Ball.

From the comments made by the others, Edward knew she had told them all about it in glorious detail. And, her description had evidently made the evening into a social event worthy of high society in Tidewater Virginia.

It was just a community dance in a small town hall, he thought.

"My Ellen and I had a *wonderful* time," she concluded. "And E.B. is *such* a gentleman!"

By the time the meal concluded with peach cobbler, made with fresh peaches shipped from Chile on ice from an Antarctic iceberg, Edward was stuffed, but no closer to figuring out how to let his hostess know he wasn't interested in marrying her. And, he certainly hadn't figured out what to do about his feelings for her daughter.

He'd just have to bury himself in his work, and try to let his unnatural feelings die from lack of stimulation.

Chapter Fifty-One

On a lovely sunny day in May, Edward read a letter from his mother that had just arrived.

The Day After Christmas, 1855
Dear Son,

We had a lovely Christmas. The church was beautiful with evergreens and candles on Christmas Eve. The whole family gathered at our home on Christmas Day to exchange gifts and, after a huge dinner, sing Christmas carols around the piano.

I must admit with sadness, it isn't the same without our sweet Eliza, and you so far away, but Lawrence seemed more himself, joking around with all the cousins, than he has since she passed away. I suppose, at nearly eighteen, one takes exuberant joy in life, no matter what twists and turns fate takes.

As of this coming January, Greencastle will make great strides in becoming a more pleasant city in which to dwell. Several ordinances have been passed, to take effect with the New Year.

The city council will impose fines for firing arms or flying kites on frequented streets, for public intoxication, for defacing monuments or playing games in a cemetery, for riding or driving a horse at more than seven miles an hour, for keeping or frequenting a house of prostitution, or being a prostitute, and for playing cricket or ball games, pitching quoits or making any loud disturbance or for opening a store on the Sabbath...

Edward looked up from his mother's letter and, shaking his head, smiled. What would she think of his life in California? He couldn't imagine ordinances like those adopted by the Greencastle City Council even being suggested, let alone enforced, in Placerville or Volcano. Not even in Sacramento or San Francisco.

Taking a deep breath, Edward knew with certainty, he would never return to live in Indiana. He was too comfortable with the lusty, zesty, lacking-in-ordinances life he led here, to be tempted to return to Greencastle.

* * *

In June, sixteen-year-old Ellen graduated from boarding school. Caroline planned a party for her and the other girls in her class. In recognition of the milestone event, she even invited several boys of the same age, from a nearby boys' school.

"You simply must come," she told Edward. "You are practically family, and Ellen would be devastated if you weren't there."

Gritting his teeth, Edward agreed to attend, determined not to let his feelings get out of control. Perhaps he'd even ask Caroline for her hand in marriage and thus make it impossible to have improper notions about Ellen.

Boots polished, shirt freshly laundered and ironed, wide-brimmed hat replaced by a bowler, he arrived at the school's assembly hall promptly at ten o'clock, carrying a large bunch of fresh flowers for the young girl graduate.

Twelve girls entered sedately and stood in their places at chairs on the stage. Dressed in white, with pastel sashes and bows, they made a delightful picture. The piano stopped playing, and to enthusiastic applause from the audience, the girls took their seats.

The two-hour program showed off the girls' individual and collective talents. They read samples of their poetry and essays on their feelings of appreciation for their school days—now over—and hopes for the future. Interspersing all this, in beautiful harmony accompanied by the piano, they sang songs of worship, patriotism, and joyful pleasures.

Edward couldn't take his eyes off Ellen. Each time she stood to speak, his heart beat faster. In her sweet voice, she showed maturity far beyond her years. The trials and hardships of the wagon train had hammered out any childish fears or doubts of her abilities. She stood before the audience, self-confident, and sweetly charming.

Edward felt enchanted, as if he were the subject of a fairytale. He couldn't help himself.

After the ceremony, when he presented the bouquet, Ellen impulsively put her arms around him and kissed him on the cheek. The touch of her arms and the feel of her kiss remained hot, as though he had been branded.

Fortunately, Caroline began organizing them to walk to the boarding house, and Ellen was taken up in the surge of young people.

Dinner went well. The girls and boys were evenly divided between two tables. White damask tablecloths, shining silverware, sparkling crystal glasses, and spring flowers in bowls made a lovely setting for the girls, who looked like bouquets of flowers as well. The more somber attire of the boys set them off perfectly.

With a pang, Edward found his place card at one table, while Ellen and Caroline were seated at the other. But then he felt a sense of relief, as he gallantly responded to the conversation of the young people, all dressed up and on their best, most mature behavior.

Caroline's parlor had a music box that played large, perforated metal disks which, with a turn of the handle, circled around and around. The boys asked girls to dance, both in the parlor and the central hall onto which the parlor door opened.

Edward danced with Caroline, and once again felt the comfortable feeling of rightness, and connection. She hummed to the music and had a dreamy, far-away look on her face.

Edward was about to say something to her, acknowledging their foreordained destiny to be together, when the music stopped. In the bustle to replace the first disk with another, and change partners as well, the moment was gone.

He watched as Ellen danced with a young boy, her eyes shining, their repartee bringing giggles to both. Edward felt a stab of loss. This was where Ellen belonged—dancing and laughing with another sixteen-year-old. Certainly not stuck with an ancient twenty-eight-year-old man like himself.

Nevertheless, Edward requested the third dance with Ellen. *After all,* he argued with himself, *she's the reason I'm here.*

She accepted with alacrity. As they waltzed around the room, Edward knew he was lost again. How could he face a future without this charming woman/child by his side?

As the dancing continued, Edward found himself with Caroline as his partner once again. As they danced, they turned out of the central hall, onto the empty front porch.

Their dancing slowed, and finally stopped, with Edward's arm around Caroline's waist.

"Caroline—" he started, just as she said, "Edward—".

They looked each other in the eyes. Edward with panic, Caroline looking sweetly understanding.

They stood that way, while the music box played in the background.

"I don't—" Edward started.

Caroline put a finger to his lips. "I know exactly what you're going to say."

"You couldn't!"

"Oh, but I do." She looked so lovely; his heart went out to her.

"You are in love with Ellen. My daughter."

Edward stood, amazed. "But… but how could you know?"

"I've k*nown* since the Christmas Ball. Perhaps even before that."

"I am," he said, feeling sad. "But, I understand it's not acceptable. I don't blame you for feeling angry with me, a man of twenty-eight going soft in the heart—soft in the head, more like it—over your precious young daughter."

"Oh, my dear, dear Edward. I don't blame you. And, I'm certainly not angry with you. In fact, I think it's a perfectly *delightful* idea!"

Edward picked Caroline up by the waist, and swung her around in a circle, right there on the front porch, where anyone walking down the street could see.

Suddenly he stopped, putting the panting, laughing woman back on her feet. "But, what will Ellen say?"

"My dear boy, Ellen has loved you since she was ten years old. She's just been terrified you wouldn't wait for her to grow up!"

Chapter Fifty-Two

Once Edward's proposal had been accepted by a joyful Ellen, and sealed with an excited kiss—the first *real* kiss she'd ever given him—he felt as though he could fly. He gave every person he met a huge smile. The sky had never been bluer, the sun more benevolent.

He was in love.

Edward couldn't believe she'd said, "Yes."

He had some difficulty getting around the fact that, just six years ago, she'd been a shy child in sunbonnet and scuffed boots walking staunchly across the American prairie. Somehow, that's how he'd always thought of her.

But now, she was a lovely lady. Young, yes. But no little girl. Today she had poise and confidence. He knew poise came from her schooling, but she'd gained her confidence crossing deserts and climbing mountains.

* * *

Edward and Ellen met with Caroline in the sitting room of the boarding house, one afternoon soon after the proposal, to do some serious planning.

"When can we get married?" Ellen asked, holding Edward's hand.

"What do you think, E.B.?" Caroline asked.

"The sooner the better, as far as I'm concerned." Edward turned and smiled at Ellen.

"Well, I've been thinking," Caroline started, paused. Turning to her daughter, she said, "I think you two need to wait at least six months—"

Ellen pouted, but she continued. "I know you fell in love with E.B. the first time you laid eyes on him, in St. Joseph, waiting for the ferry to cross the Missouri River."

Ellen smiled and nodded agreement.

"But you were a little girl, and it was a childish infatuation. You have matured, and I feel you need some time—not a lot, mind you—but a few months, to let your feelings catch up with the rest of you.

"Edward needs, and has every right to expect, a *woman* for a wife. You need to learn how to cook, shop, care for a home. And what better place to do that, than helping me here in the boarding house?" Caroline leaned over to pat Ellen's hand. "And, you'll need some time to assemble your trousseau."

Then she turned to Edward. "And you will need some time to change your perception of your bride from child to woman as well. She doesn't need a father. Or a big brother. She needs a husband. And, in my heart of hearts, I believe, given a little time for adjustment, you will be that man."

"I've waited twenty-eight years for the perfect wife." Edward smiled. "I suppose I can manage to wait another six months, or so..."

He paused, and gave Caroline a serious look. "There's just one other thing. What will I call *you?* I've thought of you as a dear and welcome friend for six years. We've been through good times and bad, as equals. I'm having much more difficulty thinking of you as my mother-in-law, than I am of realizing Ellen is to be my wife.

"Somehow, I can't quite imagine calling you 'Mother Gould.' The name is *much* too old for you. Would you mind terribly if I continued to call you Caroline?"

Feeling anxious, Edward watched her face. There was a bit of a pause.

At last she smiled and said, "'Caroline' has done very well up to now. I see no reason to change it."

Chapter Fifty-Three

June 15, 1856

Dear Family,

I have great news! I am engaged to be married!

You will recall my mentioning Ellen, whose stepfather Gould, died of cholera on the trail to California. You'll also remember Caroline, her mother, who became a dear friend from the very beginning in Saint Joseph.

Well... with Caroline's blessing, and her daughter's joyful acceptance, Ellen and I will be wed in a few months' time. Quite possibly at the beginning of the new year.

I hope you will be as happy for us, as are we here in California. I suspect you may think the difference in our ages should be a stumbling block—even though older men often do marry much younger women.

While it is true, when we met Ellen was a delightful child of ten, since then she has grown up into a most charming young woman. I wish you were here, so you could see for yourselves how perfect a wife she will be.

But now we come to the news you probably expect, but dread. Ellen and I will not be coming back to Greencastle. Nor would we expect you to come to California. The trip is long and arduous. As for us, California is our home. My memories of Greencastle and family are dear to my heart, but life here—different in many ways both subtle and obvious—is what we are now used to.

It pains me to think, in all probability I will never again see your loving faces. You must know I think of you—pray for you all—each and every day.

I cling to the thought that the future is indeed unknowable, and the possibility still exists, we shall see each other on this side of heaven. And if not, we shall surely embrace on the other side of those pearly gates.

With joy in my heart, I remain,

Your loving son,

E.B.

Chapter Fifty-Four

On July sixth, Placerville suffered a devastating fire. As soon as word reached Volcano, Edward grabbed a horse and rode as hard as he could. *Oh, my God!* he thought, desperation making his heart pound, *what of my house? What if it's burned down?*

He felt far too emotionally attached, to be an objective newspaper journalist. He liked Volcano just fine, but Placerville had been his first California home, and it broke his heart to think of the destruction the fire would cause.

His first sight of Main Street was even worse than he had imagined—the carnage complete. Every tent, every lumber building, every log cabin—gone. Nothing left but black smoldering stumps. Here and there a brick chimney stuck, like a lone sentinel, into an empty sky. Dead ashes lay, a thick carpet of grey, swirling up with every breath of breeze.

The air smelled of burnt wood, pricking Edward's nose and stinging his eyes. His horse twitched its mane and shivered with nervousness. It pawed the ground in alarm at the smell of fire.

Shaking his head in dismay, Edward had a hard time believing his eyes. There was simply nothing left of the downtown area. Building after building, including the office of the *Mountain Democrat*—gone. The press Springer had sold to Gelwicks and January—melted into a grotesque pile of molten lead. The post office burned to the ground. Letters, lovingly written, carried safely across the continent—destroyed.

Only the Tallman Soda Works survived. Built in 1835, its two-foot-thick brick walls, suitable for keeping ice, gave it the protection needed to withstand the holocaust.

Buildings and trees around the perimeter of the fire had been scorched black. Heart in his throat, Edward rode up to see if his house had survived. With a wave of relief that made him dizzy, he saw both the house and the church next door, still standing. Soot and ashes had made a dirty mess of them, but the structures remained. *Hallelujah! Thank you, God.*

Returning to the gulch, Edward found people picking through the rubble of Main Street.

"Well, that's the end of Placerville," said Nugent, shaking his head.

"Why do you say that?" asked Edward.

"It's over," Armour, the butcher agreed with Nugent. "The Gold Rush is over, and Placerville's finished."

"Towns can be rebuilt," Edward argued.

"But the Gold Rush is finished," Armour repeated. "You know the surface gold is gone. It was gone by the time you arrived, back in 1850."

"So, do I write the newspaper headline—*Placerville's Demise?*

Studebaker joined the conversation. "Things have changed since you left, E.B. When you were here, two or three men could dig a hole, follow a vein a few feet down. Now the ditches have turned into tunnels—"

"Deep ones, burrowing under the town," Armour interrupted again. "Now it takes a whole company of men to dig and shore up the sides and ceilings."

"People were beginning to leave Placerville even before you went to Volcano," Studebaker reminded him. "Now, with this fire, everyone else will leave, too. Placerville will turn into a ghost town."

"It sounds to me, as though you think the town is doomed," Edward said. "Aren't *any* of you staying?

Another man, one whom Edward didn't recognize, argued, "If we could get named the El Dorado County Seat, take it away from Coloma, we could rebuild, but this time with rock and bricks."

"If we did," Armour said, "we'd have to make Main Street wider. And straighter."

"And mark off real blocks and side streets," the man said. "Placerville could come back even bigger and better!"

"But," Studebaker's voice rang out, "it wouldn't be feasible, unless we could become the county seat. And Coloma will fight that tooth and nail. After all, its future is as dependent on being county seat as is ours."

"Volcano is betting its future on taking the Amador county seat from Jackson," Edward contributed. "That's why they backed having our newspaper there—to bolster their chances."

"But, how are they planning to get the legislature to move the county seat there?" asked Armour.

"Springer is working on starting a Democrat Club," Edward replied. "They want to send precinct delegates to the September Convention in Jackson. If he can get our delegates among the ten elected to attend the State Convention, he figures we might have a chance."

"Well, it *might* work," Armour conceded.

"I don't know how well organized and determined Jackson is," Studebaker said, "but I've *lived* in Coloma, and believe me, there's no way in hell they're going to roll over and play dead."

"I wish you well," Edward said. "After all, I consider Placerville my hometown, too. This is going to be a heart-wrenching story for me to write."

He rode once more, up the hill, to gaze at his house. He loved this, his first real home. But of what value would it be if Placerville was doomed to extinction? The business district burned. Gold, the main source of revenue, mined out.

He'd dreamed of returning here some day. Of bringing Ellen to this house as his wife. But if Placerville didn't rebuild, and Volcano didn't get the county seat, where would they live? How would he make a living? By himself he could live in a rented room, a shack, or a tent. But, he had a bride to consider.

Doubts made his heart turn to ice.

Chapter Fifty-Five

Edward noticed a flower shop nearby, on his way to visit Ellen. It had probably been there forever, but he'd never seen it before.

I bet Ellen would like some flowers, he thought. *Why not?* He smiled. *We're engaged.*

A few minutes later he rang Caroline's doorbell, two-dozen, bright-red roses clutched in one hand. Ellen, wrapped in a large, ruffled apron opened the door and gasped.

"You... you brought me roses! They *are* for me, aren't they? Not mother?"

At Edward's nod, Ellen's brown eyes danced; her cheeks flushed pink. "I... I've never had a beau bring me flowers before."

She stood on tiptoe and gave Edward a kiss. A very adult kiss. His lips warmed at the touch.

As Ellen took her bouquet into the kitchen to find a vase, Caroline hung Edward's duster and bowler on the coat tree in the vestibule.

"That was sweet of you," she said. "But you needn't have done it. You don't have to win her heart. It's already yours."

"I know, but it pleasures me to please her." He realized, with absolute clarity, there was no one he'd rather be with, than Ellen. And, nothing he'd rather do, than see what he'd just seen in her glance and blush.

"Even though we got betrothed before I could woo her, I figure every young lady deserves a bit of romantic courtship," he said.

Caroline got a far-away look in her eyes. "You may be right," she murmured.

He knew she was thinking about Ellen's father.

Oh, he wasn't the heart-stopping love of my life, she'd said of Gould... *That was Ellen's daddy... Lord, Lord, I couldn't go through losing the likes of him more than once in a lifetime...*

Edward had eaten dinner at Caroline's quite frequently over the years. He was well acquainted with the men sitting at her dining room table. But, that had been when Ellen was still in boarding school.

Now as he took his chair, he was joining them as Ellen's beau. He glowed with pride at the envious looks he received.

❊ ❊ ❊

For the next step in Edward's courtship of Ellen, he invited her and Caroline to Volcano for the weekend. They arrived by carriage on Saturday afternoon. They had tea as soon as they were ensconced in Mrs. Walker's Bed and Breakfast.

"My, my," Ellen said, sipping daintily from a flowered china cup, "who would have thought, as we trudged through that smelly Humboldt Sink, that I'd ever be having a proper

English tea? I can't believe I'm eating cucumber finger sandwiches, fresh strawberries and clotted cream, and just look at those petit fours!"

My dear, sweet Ellen, Edward thought, *what a cruel childhood you've had. It's amazing you survived. But, you did, and just look at you now.*

"It is my intention to spoil you completely," he said, "to make up for the teas you never had, growing up with your dollies."

Later that night, they attended a play in the Volcano Theatre. It was an English farce, complete with mistaken identities, people coming and going, bumping into each other at the most inopportune moments, completely misunderstanding what the other was about.

Edward enjoyed watching Ellen and Caroline laughing and clapping, as much as he enjoyed the action on the candle-lit stage.

The next morning the three of them attended church. As Edward entered, Caroline on one arm, Ellen on the other, he gave a thankful prayer for Nugent, who had made sure he found his way back to God's church.

That made Edward remember Eliza with a sharp pang of sadness. *I'll tell our children about being descendents of the great king, Charlemagne,* he vowed. *I'll call each of our daughters, "princess." And each time I do, I'll think of you.*

✻ ✻ ✻

As the engagement period continued, Edward and Ellen spent the hot, humid summer hours in Sacramento, boating on the American River or having leisurely picnics in the shade of oak trees on the banks rising high above. While they feasted on cold chicken, baking soda biscuits, fresh fruit, and chocolate cake, they talked about how much life they had already shared, and dreamed about their future.

"We'll have a house," Ellen murmured. Then, sitting up she said, "We *will* have a house, won't we?"

Kissing her on the nose, Edward reminded her, "We already have a house—in Placerville."

She smiled, and snuggled into his arms. "You know, I can hardly remember ever having lived in a house. I do so want to have a family—and live together—in a house."

After the Placerville fire, Edward wasn't so certain of someday returning to his home there. He wasn't as confident as he had been before, of where they would live—or how.

"Don't worry, my love." Ellen sat straight and tall. "We can live anywhere." She looked him in the eye. "You can do anything—publish a newspaper, work in a post office, drive a stagecoach—and... and anything else you set your hand to. If we can't live in your house in Placerville, we'll just have to live in another house, in some other town!"

Edward marveled at her resiliency, but then recalled how she had walked through the desert all night long, with precious little water. And, she'd been only ten at the time.

❋ ❋ ❋

As his floral gifts turned from roses and daisies of summer to gladiolas and chrysanthemums of autumn, they began to seriously plan their wedding.

Edward, Ellen, and Caroline sat on the boarding house porch, enjoying the gentle autumn breeze.

"Will the wedding be here in Sacramento?" Edward asked.

He felt Ellen, sitting next to him, quiver with excitement.

Caroline looked thoughtful, and then smiled sweetly. "You can have your wedding anywhere you want it. Sacramento, Volcano—I don't suppose Placerville's rebuilt enough yet..."

Ellen giggled. "Too bad we can't have it on the banks of the Sweet Water River at Devil's Gate. I could say my vows barefoot." She shook her head in wonder. "I can still remember how wonderfully cool it felt."

"And," Edward added, "I can still remember how jealous I was that all the girls and women could go wading, and none of the men did. My feet were burning inside my old, worn boots."

"Well," Caroline said, "think about it. Look around. Don't decide until you've found the place that reaches out to you and says, 'Get married here!'"

And so, the two of them spent many happy hours that fall, searching the Mother Lode for the perfect place to be wed.

They visited the small towns south of Placerville—Diamond Springs, Eldorado, Plymouth, Drytown, Sutter Creek, Jackson, and Mokelumne Hill—all of which had been on Edward's stagecoach route.

Then one balmy autumn day, Edward and Ellen stopped in the small town of Clarksville for a refreshing drink of cold apple cider. Approximately half way between Placerville and Sacramento, they'd ridden through Clarksville several times, but had never before stopped. In 1849, a man named Morgan had built a rough tavern called Mormon Tavern. But, by 1855, there were four hotels scattered around the area. Clarksville had originally been called Clarkson's Village, for the man who had established a stopping place not far from Mormon Tavern.

"I thought all of the Mormons went to Salt Lake City," Ellen said. "Was it the Gold Rush that brought you here?"

"No, not the Gold Rush," Morgan said. "We were here several years before Marshall's discovery."

Now, Edward was curious. "So, how *did* you happen to be in California?"

"You were right, thinking we came to Salt Lake City. And while we were there, we were pretty self-sufficient. We could grow food enough, and make do with what we could produce. Bartering worked well for us, but we had no source of cash money.

"Then the Mexican-American War started in 1846. America didn't have enough men on the southwestern frontier to challenge the whole Mexican army. So a call went out to any man willing to join the American army. Each one would be given a cash payment for his service. When our elders heard that, we were asked to volunteer, and several of us did."

"What was it like? Ellen asked, her eyes wide. "The war, I mean."

"Well, Miss, I can't rightly say. By the time we were outfitted and taught to fight, the war was over. It was 1848, and we were here in California, which was an independent republic at the time. The prospects looked good," he shrugged his shoulders, "so we stayed."

"Come to think of it," Edward interjected, "the man who sent out word of the California Gold Rush was a Mormon!"

"Yup," Morgan replied. "Good old Sam Brennan, owner of the *Sacramento Star* newspaper."

"E. B., this would be a perfect place to get married!" Ellen said, with an excited smile. "There's a church here, and we could spend our wedding night in one of the hotels."

"It's close enough to Placerville and Sacramento to be convenient for our friends from there to come," Edward commented. "But, I think the Springer's, and some of the others from Volcano might have to spend a night or two at one of the hotels. Hopefully they won't mind."

Ellen was nearly bouncing on tiptoes with excitement. "Let's go look at the church. See if we can talk to the pastor there. Find out if he's willing to marry us!"

Chapter Fifty-Six

January 1, 1857

Edward thought his heart might burst from happiness, as he stood next to Springer, his best man, in the tiny church in Clarksville. The Reverend Mister King, open Bible in his hands, completed the group. Outside the windows, the groom saw bare tree branches reaching into a cold, intensely blue sky. Inside, a pot-bellied stove did its best to radiate heat.

"Well," Edward murmured to Springer, "we waited *almost* six months!"

Caroline sat in the front row, looking both elated and weepy. Mary Springer sat next to her with two-year-old Thomas on her lap.

We're a small family, Edward thought, missing his parents and Lawrence, *but my folks couldn't come all this way, for the wedding. Especially in the middle of winter.*

Just then, there was a bustling at the church door. The minister's wife started playing *Here Comes the Bride* on the piano. The guests, mostly school friends of Ellen's and their families, turned to watch.

Eight-year-old Grant Springer walked gravely down the aisle, carrying a pillow with two wedding rings pinned to it.

As he approached them, he gave Edward a huge smile of pride mixed with relief that he'd arrived safely. Edward returned the smile, and placed an approving hand on his shoulder as the boy turned to face the congregation.

Next came Mary Kate, Ellen's best friend from school, as maid of honor. She looked young and properly impressed. Edward knew she was jealous of Ellen for already having found a husband. She carried a bouquet of fresh flowers Edward had ordered shipped to San Francisco from South America.

At last, the piano paused dramatically, before continuing in a new key. Everyone stood with rustling and murmurs.

And there was Ellen, looking gorgeous in her white lace gown, carrying a large bouquet, her hand on Nugent's arm. He was the closest thing either of them had to a father, here in California. He looked as pleased as punch, and she… well she radiated love. Pride. Self-assurance.

Nugent handed Ellen to Edward, and then sat on the other side of Caroline.

Edward tucked Ellen's arm in his, wanting nothing more than to pull her into a bear hug, and kiss her until she grew faint. He could tell she wanted the same thing, but they stood primly—facing the preacher—more than ready to become man and wife.

"Dearly beloved friends," Reverend King intoned, "we are gathered together here in the sight of God, and in the face of this congregation, to join together this man and this woman in holy matrimony…"

Edward and Ellen managed to say, "I do," and "I will," at the appropriate times. Flowers were handed to the maid of honor, rings unpinned from Grant's pillow, blessed by the minister, and lovingly placed on the correct fingers.

After a lengthy prayer, everyone said, "Amen."

Reverend King said in a stentorian voice, "I now pronounce you man and wife."

Then, finally, Edward kissed Ellen, perhaps a bit longer than was absolutely necessary, but not nearly as long as they would have liked.

"Ellen, my love," he said quietly, just to her, "I will love you, protect you, honor and respect you, for as long as we both shall live."

Epilogue

Pacific Grove, 1920

"You do remember!" Ellen exclaimed. "And so do I."

"And it *does* seem just like yesterday." Edward smiled.

The late afternoon fog had rolled in from the ocean, bringing a chill to the air. At some point during their long journey down memory lane, they had moved into the living room. A small fire burned cheerfully, illuminating the white, pressed metal ceiling, making the room warm and cozy.

"What else will you tell the newspaper editors' convention?"

"That's pretty much everything," Edward said. "They're only interested in the Gold Rush Era. It was such a dramatic beginning for the state."

"You should tell them about moving the paper to Jackson."

Edward cocked his head and thought. "You're right, I should! Especially since the *Jackson Ledger* is still in circulation there, after all these years."

"Volcano had such high hopes of becoming the county seat," Ellen mused. "But Jackson was too strong politically to allow the county seat to be taken away. And now Jackson is a real city."

"And Volcano's almost a ghost town," Edward added. "Simply a nice place to go for a Sunday drive."

"But, Placerville did well," Ellen said. "Took the county seat from Coloma—"

"And," Edward interrupted, "Now *Coloma's* a ghost town."

"If the editors want drama," Ellen commented, "you should tell them about driving the stagecoach with Horace Greeley as a passenger."

Edward smiled. "Yes I should. After all, Greeley was a newspaperman. Editor of the *New York Tribune* at the time. He made the trip all the way to California by stagecoach, in support of building the transcontinental railroad."

Ellen smiled. "Mark Twain wrote about Hank Monk driving Greeley the last leg of the journey to Placerville—on time for his speaking engagement—in his book *Roughing It.*"

"Because of that," Edward said, "I'm sure Monk's is the only name that will ever be in the history books. But I *did* drive the stagecoach Greeley was in. When I reached the end of my run, I handed the coach and its passengers over to Monk. And the rest really *is* history.

Edward gazed into the fire, mesmerized by the dancing flames. "As far as I know, I'm the last of the four hundred men who at one time drove stage on the overland route."

They sat, quietly remembering. "Ellen, my dear," Edward took her hand in his, "this has been an amazing life. And the fact that you've lived it with me, is simply extraordinary. I couldn't have had a better wife. Or friend."

Author's Note

It came as some surprise to me, to realize that the unexpected romance and marriage of Edward to Ellen was the climax of his Gold Rush years, and therefore the end of my story. But, I had notebooks filled with other episodes I wanted to write. This, then, is a short version of what happened after the wedding.

Edward Brochenbrough Daingerfield and Ellen Frances Logan were married eight days before her seventeenth birthday.

Her predictions for him became reality. Edward did, indeed, live in several Northern California towns and he worked at many different jobs.

On May 2nd and 9th of 1857, the following advertisement appeared in the *Jackson Weekly Ledger:*

> "For Sale" The undersigned offers for sale his interest, (being one-half) in the *Weekly Ledger* printing establishment. Declining health is my sole reason for offering to sell, as the concern is doing a prosperous and increasing business. Address: E. B. Daingerfield.

Since E. B. lived another apparently robust 67 years, I wonder if some sort of disagreement between him and Thomas Springer might have caused Edward to sell out.

Edward's father, Lawrence Lewis Butler Daingerfield died soon after that, on November 2, 1857, age 58. The eulogy printed in the *Jackson Weekly Ledger* ended with, *...when, after a tedious and painful illness, Death closed the scene around him, so calm and easy was the passage of his soul from earth to Heaven that those who watched around his dying couch scarce could tell the moment when his immortal spirit, released from its prison, took its flight for the regions of eternity.*

* * *

Ellen and E.B. had a total of seven children. The birth of their first child, Laura, on December 26, 1857, near Folsom, was announced in the *Weekly Ledger.*

In 1858 Edward moved his family back to Placerville, where he was a ditch agent for the South Fork Canal Company at Coon Hollow. Later he drove for a pioneer stage company, continuing during the Civil War, until the railroad was completed.

They had four more children during that time: Francis (Frank) born in 1859, Lawrence (Lee) in 1861, William in 1863, and Grace Gertrude (my great-grandmother) in 1864.

Over the years, the Daingerfield's experienced a lot of history being made. On April 3, 1860, the legendary Pony Express began service between St. Joseph, Missouri and Sacramento, California, with a much-heralded stop in Placerville. On October 24, 1861, Justice Stephen J. Field of

California transmitted the first transcontinental telegraph message to President Lincoln.

On May 10, 1869 a golden spike was driven at Promontory, Utah, marking the completion of the first transcontinental railroad in the United States.

E.B. and Ellen, having journeyed to California walking next to their covered wagons, must have been amazed at the newly found ease and speed of transportation and communication. Edward, who had sorted mail that had taken several months to get to Placerville, was surely astounded at how quickly letters now arrived.

Edward's younger brother, Lawrence, did have his own adventure, fighting in the Civil War. He served as a lieutenant in Indiana's *Marion Guards,* formed on August 18, 1863. Sometime after the Civil War, he must have immigrated to California, because he is buried in the Daingerfield family plot in Gilroy.

Meanwhile, starting in 1868, E.B. worked in railroading in San Francisco and San Jose for several years. The 1870 census lists Edwin and Ellen, along with children Laura 12, Frank 10, Lawrence 8, William 6, and Grace 5, "at school," and Caroline Gould, age 51 all living in the same house in Gilroy.

Edward was Gilroy's postmaster from 1875 to 1882. Their last two children were born during this time: Charles Lucius (Lou) in 1878 and Edith in 1881.

Meanwhile, in Boston, on March 10, 1876, Alexander Graham Bell's assistant, heard Bell say, "Mr. Watson, come here. I want to see you," on the world's first successful telephone conversation. Imagine, being able to actually talk to someone who wasn't in the same room!

From 1882 to 1887 E.B. was in charge of the water system at San Quentin Prison. Then he served in the State Treasurers' Office for four years. He became Pacific Grove's postmaster under President Cleveland from about 1890 to 1894.

Edward and Ellen's daughter, Grace Gertrude Daingerfield (my great-grandmother) married William R. Pyle in Gilroy, on February 1, 1886. William's father had also come to California during the Gold Rush. He came overland, while his wife Mary Mack Pyle came across the Isthmus of Panama with her two young children, Darius and Laura. I borrowed her story for the passengers on E.B.'s first stagecoach trip as driver.

The United States began building the Panama Canal on May 4, 1904. On April 18, 1906 a devastating earthquake struck San Francisco, followed by raging fires. About 700 people died.

Edward and Ellen's son, William, was lost at sea on October 29, 1903, when the steamer *Discovery* left Yakuta, Alaska, never to be seen again. On May 18, 1912, their son Lou, graduated from the University of California, Berkeley, with a degree in dentistry.

Grace and William Pyle had one son, Kenneth Daingerfield Pyle, my grandfather. He graduated from Stanford University as a mining engineer. He met my grandmother, Bertha Marie Robson Pyle, at Stanford where she worked for a professor, and also took some classes.

Interestingly enough, they married, using slightly fictitious names, in San Francisco in 1912, while my grandfather had a summer job there with Pacific Coast Steel Works. My guess is, they eloped. They married again, officially, on February 1, 1913. (My grandmother must have insisted on a 'legal' marriage when she discovered she was pregnant.) My mother, Grace Marie Pyle, born October 10, 1913, was named after her grandmother, Grace Gertrude Daingerfield.

Edward B. Daingerfield died on, July 23, 1921, age 93 years, three months and six days. His obituary said, *It was here* (Pacific Grove) *in a cozy little cottage by the sea that his latter years were spent with his loved ones, in his garden of flowers, while his thoughts often traveled back over the years that had flown, and to the places in the foothills, where as a young man, he spent many happy days.*

Ellen lived another five years, dying on June 28, 1926 at age 86. Three of her seven children survived her: Lee Daingerfield of Pacific Grove, Dr. C. L. Daingerfield of Stockton, and daughter Edith Daingerfield.

Edith Daingerfield never married. She lived with her parents, and then mother, in Pacific Grove before moving to San Francisco, where she lived in a residence for single ladies and played a mean hand of bridge.

While my grandfather was working for Homestake Mining Company of Lead, South Dakota, in a gold mine they owned in the Andes Mountains of Peru, my mother attended school in a convent in Lima. She left there, all by herself, to attend Long Beach (California) Polytechnic High School.

My mother graduated and entered UCLA at age 15. She turned 16 the next month, on October 10, 1929, just before the great stock market crash. While she was a student at UCLA, she met my father, Byron John Ellerbrock. They sat next to each other in a psychology class. He had a broken foot, and was on crutches, so Mom carried his books for him. My dad had come to California from Freemont, Nebraska, with his widowed mother. She died of breast cancer while he was still a student at UCLA.

E.B. Daingerfield must have told his children about being descendents of the great medieval king, Charlemagne, because Great-Great-Aunt Edith was motivated to research our family genealogy. She managed to trace the family all the way back to Charlemagne, and even farther back, to that king's earliest recorded ancestor, Pepin de Vain.

Her nephew, my artist/engineer grandfather, drew a family tree based on her research. He drew it like a real tree, with Charlemagne forming the trunk; the king's ancestors, Pepin de Vain, Charles Martel, Pepin the Short and all, were drawn in the roots of the tree, which is over four feet long. As a little girl, I loved finding my name and birth date on the topmost branch.

My grandfather also typed up his Aunt Edith's notes, single-spaced, using a manual typewriter, on onionskin paper, making carbon copies by inserting sheets of carbon paper, and hand-binding them into booklets. The family tree and booklets inspired me to finish researching our family genealogy. With computers and professional help, I have completed what they started. Our family's oral tradition is true. While many of the details have changed with modern research, we *are* descended from Charlemagne.

Thanks to the inspiration of Great-Great-Aunt Edith Daingerfield's research, and my grandfather's family tree and booklets, I have been able to write five novels starting with the bottommost root of Charlemagne's ancestors and ending with this, my great-great-grandfather's story of coming to California during the Gold Rush.

Because of them, I am now a member of the Order of the Crown of Charlemagne; the Conejo Valley Chapter, Daughters of the American Revolution (DAR); and the First California Company, Jamestowne Society; which in 2007 celebrated the 400th anniversary of the founding of Jamestown.

Diana M. Johnson
billndi@verizon.net